# ABILENE AMBUSH

## A HUCK CLEMONS WESTERN: BOOK ONE

### SCOTT HARRIS

# 1

## ALLEY

HUCK AND SARAH were walking down Cheyenne's main street when Huck first thought he heard something. He wasn't sure what it was, or even if he'd really heard anything. It had that same distant feeling you have in the brief moments between a dream and waking up.

But Huck was fully awake and the second time left no doubt. It was a woman screaming.

"Help! Please, help me!"

Huck and Sarah had just arrived at their hotel and Huck quickly pushed Sarah inside the front door, yelling as he turned and ran toward the scream, "Don't leave the hotel until I get back!"

He raced to the corner of the hotel, less than a hundred feet from the front door, and turned down an alley lit only by the full moon. At the far end of the alley, he saw a man standing over a woman he'd shoved up against the brick wall of the hotel.

The wall had no windows and neither did the wall on the opposite side. The walls were about ten feet apart and the alley was pretty much empty except for some scattered trash and the two people at one end and Huck at the other.

The woman screamed again, though weaker than she had before and Huck yelled out, "What the hell are you doing? Let that woman go!"

The man stood up and Huck saw right away that he was a tall, thick man, standing at least six foot four and weighing close to two hundred and fifty pounds. He saw Huck running toward him, so he took off running too, letting the woman slump to the ground.

Huck wanted to chase the man but knew his first responsibility was to the woman. When he reached her, she was alive, but barely. As he looked down, he saw a knife sticking out of her stomach. The blood had already soaked her tattered dress, which was the only thing she was wearing against the bitterly cold night. He dropped to his knees and saw that she'd been stabbed at least twice and maybe more.

Huck had seen enough stab wounds to know the woman wasn't going to make it and probably had very little time left. He sat next to her and put her head in his lap, trying to offer some comfort, while keeping his Remington

1858 pistol in his right hand and eyes peeled in case the man returned.

The woman rolled her head and looked up at Huck. He could tell right away she knew she was dying. Her breathing was rapidly becoming shallow and blood was coming out of her mouth with each labored breath. Huck leaned down as the woman struggled to say something. As she did, Tom James came racing around the corner, followed by Jimmy Huckaby and Harry Wheeler.

Tom was Huck's best friend, Huckaby was Sarah's father, and Harry Wheeler was Huckaby's best friend. They were all travelling together from Abilene to their new ranch just outside of Yellowstone in Montana Territory. Sarah was Huck's fiancée and Huck imagined she was still at the hotel with Madeline (Maddie) Stawarski, who was Jimmy's fiancée.

The six of them had stopped in Cheyenne, planning to stay for a couple nights. It was almost halfway between Abilene and Yellowstone, and after three weeks on the trail, the thought of a soft bed and different food had sounded good to everyone.

They had a late meal together, after catching a show at the town theater. The show had been good, better than the food. Huck and Sarah had been walking behind the others, so they were still on the boardwalk even though the others had stepped inside the hotel lobby.

As the three men ran up, Huck yelled out, "Big man

wearing a big hat. No more than two minutes ahead of you. Took off running when I showed up. Stabbed this woman, more than once."

Harry turned toward Jimmy and Tom. Harry had been the sheriff in Abilene until he quit to follow his friend to Montana Territory, but years of sheriffing had trained him to react quickly.

"Tom, you stay with Huck in case he comes back. Jimmy, let's go."

Without waiting for a reply, Harry took off running and Jimmy, with one last glance at the woman and Huck, followed him.

Tom had his gun out and kept scanning the alley from front to back. Without looking down, he asked Huck, "She gonna be okay?"

Before Huck could answer, four men, drawn by the commotion and a desire to help, came running around the same corner Huck had first turned down. Tom started to raise his gun, but quickly realized they were there to assist, so he holstered his gun.

The men pulled up, saw Huck and the woman, and asked the same thing Tom had. "Is she gonna be okay?"

Huck took another look at the woman, but he'd felt the breathing stop and already knew. He gently pulled the knife from her stomach, looked up at Tom and the newcomers and answered, "She will not. She's dead. And I saw the man who did it."

One of the men offered his coat and Huck placed it gently under her head before standing. As he did, he slipped the knife inside his coat. Another of the men took charge and started barking orders. He turned and faced the other three men who had come with him.

"Porter, you get the doc."

"But Luke..."

"No buts. Go get the doc and tell him to get here right away. She ain't dead 'til doc says she's dead. Logan, you get some blankets so we can cover her up and Reid, go get Marshal Hoskins. Get on now, hurry up."

The three did as they were told and the remaining man turned to Huck and Tom. "Name's Johnson. Luke Johnson. Now, what happened here?"

Huck looked at Tom and then at Luke and said, "Best wait 'til the marshal gets here. Hoping to only have to tell this once."

Luke didn't appear to like the answer and struck Huck as someone used to getting what they ask for. He started, "Son, I think you should tell me..."

This time it was Tom who spoke.

"Mr. Johnson. My friend said we'll wait for the marshal, so that's what we're gonna do. Your friends took off running, so it shouldn't be long."

Just as Johnson started to speak again, the man named Reid, along with a man Huck and Tom assumed to be the marshal, came around the corner. Johnson, with a nasty look at Huck and Tom, turned and started walking toward them.

When he did, Tom whispered to Huck, "What'd she say? Right at the end there, I saw her try and talk. What'd she say to you?"

"I'm not sure, but it meant something to her."

# 2

## MARSHAL

CHEYENNE WAS A SMALL TOWN, founded six years previously in 1867. The Union Pacific Railroad had picked the location to be the headquarters for the railroad they planned to build in that part of the country. As the same time that announcement was made, the United States Army announced they would build a fort to protect the railroad and all that would naturally and inevitably grow up around it.

When the trains started running later that year, Cheyenne boomed and became known as the 'Magic City of the Plains.' The following year, 1868, the United States formally recognized the Territory of Wyoming, adding fuel to the already raging growth fire.

Huck knew none of that, just that a woman had died in

his arms, stabbed to death by a man he got a decent look at and whose knife he had hidden inside his heavy coat. Jimmy and Harry returned, out of breath, but without the killer.

The marshal walked up with Reid, said hello to Johnson and asked, "What the hell happened here?"

Johnson started to speak, but Huck cut him off.

"You the marshal here?"

"I am. Marshal Hoskins, Dan. And you?"

"Name's Huck. Huck Clemons. The other men here, the ones you don't know, are my friends. I saw the murder and I saw the murderer."

"Tell me what you saw."

Before Huck could answer, former sheriff Harry Wheeler jumped in.

"Marshal, my name's Harry Wheeler. Up until a couple a weeks ago, I was sheriff down in Abilene, Kansas. Thinking maybe before Huck tells you what he saw, might be a good idea to move to your office."

The marshal, clearly not happy with Huck or now Harry, or probably anyone who didn't do exactly what he wanted, gruffly asked, "Why?"

Harry leaned forward and said, "Fewer people hear his story, better chance you have of solving this crime. Best the whole town doesn't know who you're looking for."

The marshal looked around at his friends, the obviously dead woman and the men he just met and begrudgingly nodded and turned back down the way he had first come. As he did, Porter and the doc came running around the corner. Without slowing down, the marshal called out, "Dead whore back there, Doc. Get it taken care of."

Huck and Harry shared surprised looks as they followed the marshal. Jimmy and Tom stayed back with the other men. The marshal's office was right around the corner and when the three men entered, the marshal closed the door against the growing cold. He took a metal cup and poured himself some coffee, savoring the first sip before taking a seat behind the big wooden desk.

Almost as an afterthought, he asked Huck and Harry if they wanted a cup. They did and each poured themselves one before taking seats on the front side of the desk.

"Now, what'd you want to tell me that you couldn't say back there?"

Huck, after a quick glance at Harry, starts, "I heard a woman yellin', so I went running toward the screams. I came around the corner, saw a man stabbing her while he had her pinned to the wall. I yelled. He dropped her and ran."

"What'd the man looked like?"

"Big man. Maybe six foot four. Every bit of two hundred and forty pounds. Heavy beard and big thick coat, mighta been buffalo."

The only thing the marshal said was, "Anything else?" but both Huck and Harry saw something pass over his face that let them know the description meant something to him. Both men would have guessed the marshal knew at least one man who matched it.

Huck waited a moment and answered, "Sound like anyone you know, Marshal?"

"It's a big town with a lotta big men. Could a been any one of 'em. Thing is, that was Fanny back there. She's just a whore at the Bucket o' Beer. No one's gonna care much that she was kilt. No one ever does."

Huck started to stand and then remembered the incident in Casper where he almost beat a man named Cactus Bill to death for insulting his mother. He took a moment, gathered himself and said, "You sayin' crimes against whores aren't crimes in your town?"

"Now, you listen to me, Hank—"

"Huck. Name's Huck."

"Okay then, Huck. This is a tough town and things happen. My job is to make sure they don't happen to the wrong people. Lotta people in this town like it that way and the ones that don't, well, hell, no one cares 'bout them anyway."

Huck thought for a moment before responding.

"I care."

"So what? It ain't your town."

"You're right, it ain't. Thing is, Marshal, the woman died in my arms. Don't care what she did for a livin', no one deserves to die that way. Stabbed and left to bleed out in a filthy alley? That ain't right. I guess what I'm sayin' is, if you don't want to look into it, I will."

Before the marshal could respond, former sheriff Harry Wheeler added, "Huck's staying? I am too. Can't stand by and watch a murder take place and not even try to find who did it. Not in my nature. Badge or not."

The sheriff leaned forward, stared at both men, then spoke. "Now, boys. You just settle down. I didn't say I wasn't gonna look into it. Maybe I will."

Huck, still fuming at the man he had immediately disliked and distrusted, stood up and said, "Maybe ain't gonna cut it. We're in a hurry to get moving, but I think I want to see how your investigation goes first. Maybe I can even help."

"Don't need your help and don't need you hanging around town, stirring things up over some old whore."

This time it was Harry who stood and very quietly spoke to the sheriff.

"Sheriff, I think I'll stay with Huck. I'm guessing we all will. We see you catch the man, or at least make an honest effort, we'll ride on. But until then…"

"Listen, both of you. This is my town. You hear me? My town. I decide who looks into what, not a couple of drifters.

Now get the hell out of my office and don't come back. This is none o' your business and it's best if you just get on your horses and keep riding."

"And if we choose to stay for a couple of days?"

"Best you don't. Best you just don't do that."

# 3

# HOSKINS

THE SHY ANNE was a decent hotel, with a restaurant on one side and a clean saloon on the other. It was fifteen minutes since Huck and Harry had left the marshal's office. The six members of the traveling party—Huck, Sarah, Jimmy, Maddie, Tom and Harry—were sitting on the restaurant side of the hotel, nursing cups of coffee and nibbling at some bread and hard cheese. No one had much of an appetite.

Jimmy broke the silence. "Harry, Huck, you say you saw something in the marshal's face. Saw it when you described the man you saw?"

Harry answered, "We did. Least I certainly did. Done my fair share a questionin' and can usually tell when a man's hidin' something, and I'd bet a twenty dollar gold piece he was."

Sarah asked. "What? What do you think he was hiding?"

Before he could answer, Jimmy spoke up, looking at Huck as he did. "Not sure Sarah and Maddie need to be here for this. They don't need to hear about no killing, 'specially of a woman... no matter what she did for a living."

Huck waited until Jimmy was done, then looked to his left at Sarah. Huck, still not eighteen years old and Sarah, a full year younger, had fallen in love in Abilene when Huck had ridden through on his way to his new home in Montana Territory.

It had taken some time to convince her father that he was serious about Sarah and a good enough man to be her husband—and that she was ready to be a wife. But when he was convinced, he decided to sell his restaurant in Abilene and move with her. Somewhere in there, he met and fell in love with Maddie Stawarski.

Then, surprising everyone, she agreed to give up her brand new teaching job and move with them, though not until she had a ring on her finger and the promise of a wedding when they got to Montana Territory.

Sheriff Harry Wheeler, tired of being a sheriff and hating to see his best friend leave, followed right along. Tom and Huck had been best friends as long as they could remember. Tom had made the return trip from Montana Territory to Abilene to help escort his friend one way and now his friend and his fiancée on the return trip.

After a long look at Sarah, Huck turned and spoke to Jimmy.

"Mr. Huckaby, I can't speak for Maddie and maybe I shouldn't be speaking for Sarah, but she should stay. What we need to talk about, well, it's not pretty, but it affects all of us, and I want to know what Sarah thinks. This trip, this life we're all gonna be leading, well, it's not easy. Don't know exactly what, or when, but tough times are coming and the best way I can protect your daughter is for her to be prepared as possible. This, tonight, well that's a part of it."

Huck could see that Mr. Huckaby didn't like that answer and wondered what would happen next. It didn't take long. Though he tried to be polite, everyone at the table could tell Jimmy Huckaby was not happy.

"Now, Huck, you listen here. I gave my blessing and I stand by that, but she's still my little girl and she's only—"

Sarah interrupted. "Only what, Father? Only sixteen?"

Jimmy started to answer, but Sarah kept right on going.

"You're right. I am only sixteen. And I know in some ways, I'll always be your little girl. I love that you want to protect me. You always have, especially since Momma died. But I'm also getting married. I'm halfway between the only place I've ever been and somewhere I never even knew about until Huck rode into town.

"But for me to be the wife I want to be, to be the woman I want to be, I can't have you trying to keep me from knowing the truth. Even when it's hard. Now, I want, I need, to hear what Huck has to say so that we can decide together what needs to be done."

Jimmy started again, "But Sarah..."

"Daddy, I'm staying. Something terrible happened tonight and like it or not, my Huck's involved. That means I'm involved. Maybe means we all are, but me and Huck, well..."

Jimmy looked around the table and found understanding, but not agreement looking back at him.

"Harry?"

"She's right, Jimmy. This is her life now and inside, you know that. She needs to be strong and keeping her in the dark isn't gonna help that happen."

"Maddie, you understand..."

"I do. I understand everything you said. I also understand what Sarah is saying. I never thought of that when I agreed to be your wife and then to move to someplace that's not even a state. I thought coming from Pittsburgh to Abilene was a huge move and maybe it was, but this is much more.

"I may be ten years older than Sarah, but she is much wiser. If I'm going to share my life with you, and I am, I need to share all of it. The good. The bad. The horrible. I'm sorry, Jimmy, but Sarah's right about staying and I am too."

Jimmy Huckaby looked confused and turned to his old friend Harry. "Harry, when did I lose control?"

Harry waited a moment before answering and then with a huge grin, said, "Jimmy. You were married, then had a beautiful daughter who is now a young woman and then she got herself engaged. Now you're fixin' to get married again. When did you ever think you were in control?"

There was a moment of silence before Jimmy shook his head and started laughing, joined quickly by the entire table.

"Okay. Okay. Now that that's been made clear, what are 'we' gonna do?"

Huck, who had watched the whole thing in amazement, leaned forward and said, "There's a couple of things I haven't told anyone yet."

# 4

## CLUES

A HUSH CAME over the table as everyone stared at Huck, especially Harry who had been with Huck when they met with Marshal Hoskins.

Harry asked, "What do ya mean, haven't told anyone yet? I was sitting with you in the marshal's office and you didn't say anything then."

"You're right, I didn't. We both agreed he was hiding something, right?"

"That's true. Way he looked. Way he acted. Didn't sit right with me."

"Well, me either. Decided right then and there it wouldn't do any good to tell him what I knew, except maybe to help him protect whoever he's protecting."

Jimmy spoke next. "You think the marshal's protecting someone?"

Huck answered, "I do. When I described the man I saw, it was clear to me he thought he knew who it was, but when we pushed him on it, he said it could describe any number of men."

Jimmy continued, "Could it?"

"Not a lot of men, but maybe more than one. He was a big man. A few inches over six feet tall and quite a few pounds over two hundred. Big, thick beard—black, I think—and he wore a large coat, probably buffalo. Can't be too many men fitting that description in a town this size."

Harry added, "Thinking about it now, it does seem like the marshal knew who Huck was talking about, or at least had a good idea. He didn't seem to be much interested in trying to find who killed her. Said no one's gonna care about a... about a woman who did her work."

Maddie, who had stayed quiet so far, jumped in and they could all hear the anger.

"Are you saying that because of her work, her life didn't count?"

Harry, who was seated across the round table from Maddie, leaned even farther back before answering.

"No. No. I did not say that. I'm saying the marshal said no one was gonna care, and he might not even bother looking into it. Truth is, I don't know if it's because he's lazy, protecting someone, or really doesn't care about women... women."

"Prostitutes. He doesn't care about prostitutes." Maddie's anger grew.

Jimmy decided to try and calm her down a bit. "Maddie, dear, I don't think I've ever seen you like this. Harry here, he's just telling us what he heard, not what he believes. If that's how the marshal feels, I don't think anyone here would agree with him."

By the looks on their faces, everyone showed their agreement with Jimmy, as well as their surprise at seeing a side of Maddie they hadn't seen before. She continued, "Well, then, what are we going to do about it?"

Jimmy, learning things about his fiancée at a fast pace, stammered, "We?"

"Yes, we. If the marshal isn't going to do anything, don't you think we should? A woman, I don't care what kind of woman. A woman was killed in a filthy alley, left to die in the night with a knife in her gut. Someone has to try and find out who did it. Now, Huck, you said you have some more information?"

Huck, still trying to understand exactly what was happening and who this new 'Maddie' was, answered, "I do."

"Well, then, let's hear it."

Tom and Harry looked at Huck, smiling, while Sarah reached across and took Maddie's hand.

Not knowing what else to do, Huck continued, "Well, as she was dying, she whispered one word to me. I think it was a name. It was hard to hear, 'cause she was fightin' for every breath, but I think she said, 'Dora.' Not sure, but I think that's what she said."

Tom asked, "Any idea who Dora is or why she gave you her name?"

"No. At first I thought it might be her name, but the marshal called her Fanny. Maybe it's her mother? Or a daughter, a friend? I don't know."

This time it was Huck's turn to be surprised as Sarah spoke.

"Well, it's something. We need to find out who Dora is."

Harry, who had been watching with slight amusement as Maddie and Sarah seemed to take control of the conversation, poured himself a fresh glass of lemonade and spoke slowly and quietly. "Ladies, I appreciate your concern for Miss Fanny. It's one I think we all share. However, we are guests in this town and the marshal made it very clear to me and Huck that our help is not only unwelcome, he'd prefer we leave sooner than later."

Maddie started to interrupt, but Harry stopped her and continued.

"I didn't say we would be leaving soon, or that we wouldn't help, but let's not rush into this. We don't know the town and we don't know the people. Maybe the marshal will have a change of heart and take this murder seriously. If he does, good. We can move on to our new lives. If he doesn't, we can decide what to do, but I need to be clear about something." He looked directly at Sarah as he continued.

"Sarah, I've known you your whole life. Couldn't love you more if you were my blood. But there's no 'we' in this, least as far as you and Maddie are concerned. I don't know what we're dealing with here, but I've done my share of looking into murders. If I've learned anything, it's that men don't fancy the idea of swinging from a rope and will do anything—to anyone—to make sure that doesn't happen.

"Whoever killed this woman is a vicious, heartless killer and if it falls on us to find him, it's gonna be hard enough. Thing is, he's already shown he's willing to kill women, so the two of you"—again, he took a long look at Sarah and Maddie—"can't be part of 'we.' Understand?"

The two women looked at each other and Harry saw the look of resigned acceptance on both their faces.

"Good. Just the way it's gotta be. Now, Huck, you said you had a couple a pieces of information. What's the second?"

Without a word, Huck reached into his coat and pulled out a knife. The men all recognized it as a Bowie knife, fully a foot long. The dried blood on the blade glistened in the lamp light.

# 5

# DK

THEY ALL STARED for more than a minute, though it seemed much longer. Some stared at Huck, some at the knife.

Sarah broke the silence. "Is that, is that the knife..."

"Yes. When the man saw me and ran, he left this knife in Miss Fanny. I pulled it out and shoved it inside my coat and forgot about it until we all sat down. I'm not sure I would have shown it to Marshal Hoskins anyway, but I didn't think of it then."

Harry picked up the knife and spoke next, "This is a twelve-inch blade. Takes a big man to wield something this heavy. Fits the description you gave, Huck. And the blood..."

Tom gestured for the knife and Harry passed it across the table to him, handle side first. Tom took a look at the knife and then they all watched as something caught his attention. Tom drew the knife closer, looked intently and then said, "Something carved into this leather handle. Crude, but it looks like 'DK.' Whadda you think that is?"

Jimmy quickly answered, "Initials. Could be the killer's initials or could be the initials of someone who owned the knife before. Man who kills a woman certainly isn't above stealing a knife. Hell, maybe even killing to get it."

Tom gave the knife back to Harry, who sat for a moment, twirling the knife absently while obviously deep in thought. They all watched and waited until he spoke.

"Huck, this is up to you. When I was sheriff, I would have expected anyone in my town to bring this knife right away and to tell me about 'Dora.' You wanna do that, I'll walk back down with you, make sure the marshal understands you just forgot about this in the heat of the moment and brought it to him as soon as you remembered. Thing is—"

Huck jumped in, "Thing is, if he's really hiding something, if he's protecting someone and we give it to him, we'll probably never see this knife again. It's certain no judge ever will."

Harry nodded. "Yep, that is the thing. I gotta tell you. I wouldn'ta taken well to someone keeping things from me when I was looking into a murder. Woulda been pretty upset and maybe begun to wonder why they were hidin' something. Maybe even started to wonder if they had something to do with the murder."

Maddie started to speak, "You mean..."

"I do. It'd be real easy for the marshal to start thinking maybe Huck had something to do with this or at least want others to think that way. Huck's the only one who even claims he saw the killer and now he shows up with the knife that he says killed her? Take a fool of a marshal to not at least consider Huck being involved."

This time it was Sarah who jumped in. "But I heard the woman scream..."

"I know you did. But you didn't see anything and you're planning on marrying Huck. I also know it's not Huck's initials on the knife. But, if me and Huck are right and the marshal is trying to protect someone, no better way to do that than to get people thinkin' it was someone from out of town."

Jimmy, deciding the evening needed a new direction, offered up to the group, "How about we all sleep on this for the night and talk about it again over breakfast? Marshal's probably gone for the night anyway and we're all tired and hungry. Let's order something to eat and talk about something, anything, other than what happened tonight. Heck, we never even had a chance to get a meal. I know I'm ready for a large steak."

It took a moment, but pretty soon everyone was nodding their agreement. Huck quietly picked up the knife and slid it back inside his coat.

As he did, Sarah reached across and took his hand.

"Jimmy's right. Nothing you can do about it now. Let's try to enjoy a meal and we can talk about it in the morning."

"Okay. Okay, let's do just that."

Jimmy, who found to his surprise he missed owning and running his restaurant, took the liberty of ordering for everyone. Twenty minutes later, two full platters were delivered to the table, brimming with steaks, pork chops, fried eggs, three different kinds of vegetables and two large loaves of bread with a tub of sweet apple butter. It was followed quickly by two full pitchers of cold milk.

The conversation stopped, or at least slowed down, as they all realized how hungry they were. Just as they were all finishing up their meals, two hot pies—one apple, one huckleberry—were delivered. Maddie cut each pie into six slices and everyone at the table got one slice of each. After weeks on the road, the pies tasted extra sweet and extra good. Tom and Harry looked on with envy as Jimmy and Huck got to finish what Maddie and Sarah couldn't.

The conversation started up again as everyone savored their dessert. Sarah asked, "How long before we get home?" She liked the sound of 'home' as she said it and it brought a smile to her face. Huck's too as he answered.

"We've got about six hundred miles left. Now that spring's here, the weather should make traveling easier, so we could be there in three weeks, four at the most. I'm excited to see what they've done since Tom and I left. Winter was supposed to be real bad, maybe the worst in years, so I guess they might still be digging out. Like we talked about before, Sarah and I, our house is done, 'cept for the decorating, which I thought best to leave for Sarah."

This brought laughter to the table and Jimmy added, "You may wind up making a good husband after all."

Huck nodded and continued, "Between our place and the main house, there's room for everyone to stay until the town is done being built. Then everyone can build their own place and figure out what they plan on doing, me and Sarah included."

Jimmy spoke again. "First thing better be you two gettin' married, or my daughter won't be staying in your place, don't care how big it is."

Before Huck could respond, Tom leaned across and grabbed his arm, whispering, "Big man just walked into the saloon. Saw him across the hotel lobby. Don't know for sure, but he could certainly be the man you described."

# 6

# BLACK

HUCK TURNED to see the man and just got a glimpse of him before he strode out of view. The glimpse was enough to let Huck know he could be the man, but before Huck could be sure, he'd moved deeper into the saloon and out of view.

Huck turned back toward Tom and said, "That could be him. Just saw him for a second, but big enough and the coat looked about right."

Harry noticed the two whispering and leaned in and asked, "What's going on here? Thought we were done with this 'til morning?"

Huck looked at Tom and shrugged, then answered, "Tom saw a man. Just came into the saloon. I only got a quick look, but it might be him. I gotta go see."

Harry started to stand, saying, "I'll go with you."

Huck placed his hand on Harry's arm and pulled him until he sat back down. "I don't think that's a good idea. People mighta seen us going in or out of the marshal's office together. I'd just as soon they didn't notice us now. Jimmy, before you say anything, you can't go. I have to, so you need to stay with your daughter and your fiancée. Make sure they get to the rooms and make sure they're safe. Tom'll go with me, and we'll meet you upstairs in a little while."

Harry and Jimmy hated it, but they knew Huck was right. The check was quickly paid and Tom and Huck headed through the hotel lobby to the saloon on the opposite side. The other four waited a couple of minutes, then headed upstairs.

It was a saloon, but a nice one, clearly different than the Bucket o' Beer. Tom and Huck found an empty table in the corner and sat, each with his back to a wall. At the table next to them, five men sat playing small stakes poker. They struck Huck as locals, just passing another night in town. They had a couple pitchers of beer on the table, but no hard liquor and spoke with the easy familiarity of men who'd done this before.

The two looked around the saloon but didn't see the man. He was too big to blend in, but before they could say anything, the man they were looking for walked in the back door, to the far right of the bar and on the opposite side of the saloon from where Huck and Tom sat.

Tom leaned over and said, "Musta been using the outhouse." Huck nodded but kept staring at the man.

He hadn't gotten a great look in the alley. It was dark and the man ran quickly when he heard Huck call out. But Huck thought, this could easily be the man. He was a huge man, bigger than Huck had thought at first. He had a full black beard, a large black hat and a buffalo fur coat that was black with age and what appeared to be a lack of interest in cleanliness. He moved through the saloon with the ease of a man who had nothing to fear and not a care in the world.

Tom started to lean toward Huck again but before he could ask, Huck answered, "I'm pretty sure that's him. Just can't be too many men who look like that. Not sure how to tell for sure, so maybe we just sit for a bit and watch?"

"Sure, Huck, whatever you say. Can't help much though, sorry."

"Just being here's plenty, Tom. Always feel safer when you're around."

Tom fought back a smile, but sat up just a little straighter, remembering a time, not so long ago, when he wasn't any good on the trail, or in a fight, and how his childhood friend had kept working with him to get better. Knowing Huck felt this way now made Tom feel better about himself, like he was finally carrying his weight.

The large man started to walk toward Huck and Tom, and Huck thought that maybe somehow he knew. Huck's hand dropped to his gun and he saw that Tom was doing the same. But the man stopped at the table with the five poker players.

One of the men looked up and greeted him, "Hey, Black. Buy you a beer?"

The large man grinned, but it was not a pleasant grin. It was the grin of a man used to getting his own way. "You can get me a pitcher and while you're doing that, I think I'll take a seat and join your game."

One of the other men looked around and said, "Gee, Black, table's full. Only seats five."

As the man designated to bring back a pitcher stood up, Black grabbed the now empty chair and sat down. For a moment, it looked like the man was going to say something, but the smile left Black's face. It was replaced with an ugly stare. Tom watched as his hand pushed back the buffalo coat, exposing a filthy shirt, two holstered guns and a knife scabbard. The man who'd given up his seat quickly looked away and headed toward the bar.

Black started playing, using the money the man had left behind. When he returned with the pitcher, he set it on the table and without even trying to retrieve his money, walked away without saying a word.

Black laughed and said, "Austin's always been a coward. Ain't stupid, though, I'll give him that. Now, I'm raisin' a dollar. Who's in?"

Tom and Huck watched as the man called Black

cleaned out the other four players in less than a half hour. It was clear they wanted nothing more than to leave and equally clear they weren't going anywhere until all the money sat in front of the grinning giant. Huck wondered if it wouldn't have been quicker for Black to have simply pulled a gun and demanded the money, but maybe he enjoyed it more this way.

When it was over, and he had all the money, he shoved back the chair, stood up, swept the money into his large hat, revealing a full head of thick black hair, laughed at the four remaining men and walked away.

When he was out of earshot, one of the remaining four men said, "Son of a bitch's been doing that at least once a month. I don't mind losing to you boys, but I hate getting robbed, 'specially by the law."

This caught both Tom and Huck's attention, as did the comment from another of the men, "Marshal's gotta do something 'bout Denny. He's just gettin' worse and worse."

With that, the four pushed back, took a final swig of their very expensive beers and headed for the door.

As soon as they were gone, Huck turned to Tom. "Did you hear that? I think he might work for the marshal. Plus, he goes by Black, but his name's Denny. That could be the 'D' in DK."

Tom nodded and added with a sense of urgency, "It's more than that, Huck. You couldn't see it from where you're sitting, but when he opened his coat, he had a knife scabbard on his left side. Big scabbard. Leather."

Huck looked at Tom. "Lots a men carry knives out here. We both do."

"This one was empty."

# 7

# DORA

WITHOUT KNOWING HE DID IT, Huck reached inside his coat and touched the knife he'd pulled out of Miss Fanny, saying to Tom as he did, "Come on, let's get back to the hotel and the girls."

They walked silently out of the saloon, through the hotel lobby to the far side, where the stairs to the second floor and the rooms were located. Both turned when the front door opened and they were surprised to see Harry walk through. Huck, immediately concerned for Sarah, started to speak, but Harry stopped him and said, "Everyone is fine. Let's go upstairs to talk."

They had taken three rooms at the end of the hall. Huck and Tom shared the first room. Harry and Jimmy had the last room, closest to the window at the end of the hall, and Sarah and Maddie shared the room in the middle, protected on both sides by the men. Harry led the two past their own room and stopped and knocked on the middle door.

A gruff voice, one they recognized as Jimmy, barked, "Who is it?"

Harry answered, "It's us."

The door opened a crack and the three men watched as Jimmy confirmed it was them and them only. Only then did he set down the Colt 45 Peacemaker that he'd bought for this trip and let them in. Sarah and Maddie were sitting safely on one of the two beds.

Huck thought back to when he first met Sarah's father in his Abilene restaurant, which was known for having 'The Best Breakfast in Abilene.' What Huck remembered, and what still scared him more than the Peacemaker, was the huge meat cleaver that Jimmy Huckaby seemed to carry everywhere. Huck was certain it was a reminder about how he expected his daughter to be treated—and what would happen to anyone who treated her unkindly.

Huck started to speak, but before he could, Harry did. "The girls were safe the whole time. No one was going to get through, Jimmy, even if they thought they had a reason to, which so far, I don't think anyone has."

Huck nodded and added, "But why did you leave anyway? Two men would have been better."

"I went down to the Bucket o' Beer."

Huck was unable to keep the surprise out of his voice.

"You did what? Why'd you go down there?"

"Got to thinking about what you said, 'bout Miss Fanny whispering 'Dora' before she died. Thought maybe it was someone at the Bucket since she worked there and it's where she was killed."

Tom asked, "And?"

"Dora doesn't just work there; she owns the place."

Tom asked again, "And?"

"I asked around. That's how I found out she owned the place. Wasn't sure what to do next. Woulda known back in Abilene, but this isn't my town and I didn't want to attract a lot of attention. I was finishing a beer and just looking around when a woman walked behind the bar and offered me another beer. Pretty gal, maybe my age and clearly used to being in charge. As she slid the beer across the bar, she said very quietly, 'Meet me upstairs, last door on the left. Finish your beer first.' Without waiting for an answer, she turned and walked away, laughing and waving at what I assume were some of her regulars.

"I figured she'd been told I was asking about Dora and either she was Dora, or she knew who was. I took my time with the beer, checking in the big mirror behind the bar to see if anyone was watching me. When I was sure no one was, I headed upstairs.

"Worked my way down to the last door on the left. Wasn't sure what I would find, so I kept my eyes open and my hand on my gun. Tapped gently on the door and heard a voice call out from inside, 'Who's there?' I said, 'It's me, the man from bar. You told me to come up.' The door opened a crack, we recognized each other and she let me in, closing and locking the door behind me before asking...

*"Heard you were asking for me?"*

*"You Dora?"*

*"I am. Why were you asking?"*

*"My name's Harry Wheeler."*

*"I know who you are."*

*"How could you..."*

*"Mr. Wheeler, it's a small town and everyone in it knows you and that boy you're traveling with..."*

*"Huck. And he's no boy. He's as much a man as anyone in this town."*

*"Meant no offense, Mr. Wheeler."*

*"Call me Harry, please."*

*"Meant no offense, Harry. Like I was saying, it's a small town and everyone knows... knows Huck saw Fanny get killed and saw who done it."*

"Here's where I asked if I could sit, 'cause I see this was going to take a while. She waved me over to one of the two stuffed leather chairs. Very comfortable. Come to think of it, the whole room was plenty comfortable and plenty fancy. Anyway, I kept talking.

*"Not surprised. I was sheriff back in Abilene and it never stopped amazing me how fast news traveled."*

*"Well, we're much smaller than Abilene, so you can imagine.*

Doesn't explain why you were asking around 'bout me though, does it?"

"I'll get to that. First, this is your place?"

"It is."

"Cleaner than most."

"We try. I like to run a safe place, for the customers and the girls. Mostly the girls. I used to be one and it's a hard enough life. Least it can be clean and safe. Or so I thought."

"Not as safe as you thought, or at least hoped?"

"It was, least it was up until about six months ago."

"What happened then?"

"One of my girls was killed. First one. Had a couple roughed up when I first started, but I had that taken care of."

"What do you mean, 'taken care of'?"

"I knew who did it and had a couple friends of mine... well, they were given a message to never return and a bit of a beatin' to go along with it. Word got out fast that I protect my girls and things stayed pretty good. Until..."

"Until one of them was killed."

"Yes."

"How was she killed?"

"With a knife."

"Same as Miss Fanny?"

Harry looked around the room and said, "That's when she said the worst part."

"Not just the same way, but Mollie, that was her name, Mollie, was killed by the same man."

# 8

# KRAMER

SARAH GASPED when she heard what Harry said and when she recovered, she asked, "Does Dora know who killed Miss Fanny?"

Harry nodded and answered, "And the first woman, too. The one from a few months ago."

Tom spoke next. "Why hasn't she gone to the marshal about this? Man should be arrested and tried."

This time Harry shook his head as he answered, "Not quite as easy as all that."

Tom pushed, "Why not?"

"As Dora said to me, 'Knowing and proving are two different things.' She believes she knows who did it. Matter o' fact, there's no doubt in her mind. But even if she's right, maybe especially if she's right, she's afraid to do anything about it."

Sarah asked, "Why?"

"There's more than one reason. For starters, she didn't see either murder. Only one who did was Huck."

Maddie asked, "If no one saw the first murder and only Huck saw the second, how does this Dora woman know?"

Harry's face flushed a bit, something Jimmy hadn't seen in their years of friendship, so he tried to figure out how to help his friend, asking, "Harry, you got things to say, things you don't wanna say in front of Sarah and Maddie?"

Harry nodded and Jimmy turned to his daughter and fiancée. "Sarah, Maddie, I heard what you said downstairs tonight, 'bout having to be tough to live where we're going to live and the way we're going to live. I think you saw that we all respected that. But I'm gonna have to ask that you do the same and don't make Harry say things that are best not said around good women. You know where he was tonight and you can see his face good as I can. Please go next door into our room and wait while we talk this through."

Sarah started to say something, but her father stopped her. "Biscuit, I know you're gettin' married, but I'm still your father and I'm tellin' you if Harry doesn't think you should hear this, then you shouldn't hear this. I'm sorry, but sometimes that's just the way it's gotta be. Now, go on next door, please, and we'll be done here soon."

Sarah and Maddie reluctantly stood up and Huck escorted them the twenty feet to the next room. No one said a word. Huck waited until he heard the lock snap, knowing there was a long and difficult conversation coming up at some point. He let himself back in the middle room and took his seat, looking at Jimmy and thinking about Maddie as he said, "This isn't going to be any easier for you than it is for me."

"I know, but we'll let that be tomorrow's problem. For tonight, we need to hear what Harry has to say."

Harry, his face back to its normal color, started, "The man Dora is convinced killed both women is a regular at her place. He's been coming since it opened. Drinks hard, sometimes scares some of the other customers away and likes to have one girl that's 'his.' Miss Fanny is the fourth girl he's laid claim to."

Huck asks, "Was Mollie one of his girls?"

"She was and there was two more before her."

Huck continued, "What happened to them?"

"First one, he slapped around a bit. Dora tried talkin' to him, but he wouldn't listen and didn't care. Girl left. Second one got beat up pretty bad. Almost died. Took three weeks before she could get outta bed and when she did, Dora gave her money to go back to Chicago, which is where she was from. Never heard from her again. He picked Mollie next, until she was killed one night. Stabbed a couple of times and left to bleed to death. She wasn't found until the next morning."

This time Jimmy asked, "If Dora knows, or thinks she knows, who did this, why doesn't she go to the marshal?"

"I'm getting there, but first there's more. This man, a very large man, has a violent temper and is quick with his fists, his knife or a gun. This is a tough town, but Dora says everyone's afraid of him. He drinks, gambles and whores quite a bit and prefers Dora's place and Dora's girls over either of the other two whorehouses in town. The thing is, and this is really why I didn't want Sarah and Maddie here... he sometimes has... sometimes when he's with the girls, he has trouble with..."

Jimmy smiled as he said, "We get it. Thanks for not bringing that up before."

Harry smiled back. "Not something I thought I'd ever be talking about. Anyway, when that happens, he gets mighty mad and blames the girls. First time, 'bout a year ago, he slapped the one girl around a bit. Didn't hurt her much, but still, enough so she left town. Then the next time, like I said, he beat the girl pretty bad. Last time, he killed Mollie and then this time, well... we all know what happened."

Huck asked, "And she's sure it's the same man all four times? Couldn'ta been anyone else?"

"It was the same man last seen with each of the four and the first two, the ones who survived, swore to Dora it was him, but they were both too scared to testify. Since he was with Mollie and Fanny the nights they were killed, yay, Dora's sure."

Huck stood up. "Well, this time, there's another witness.

I'll sure as hell swear out a warrant with the marshal. I'll stay here until the judge arrives and give my testimony. Will Dora give you his name?"

"She already did."

"Let me guess. His first name is Denny?"

Harry, surprised that Huck knew that, answered, "It is. Least that's what Dora said. Denny Kramer. Goes by Black mosta the time."

Tom looked across at Huck, saying, "Then it's the same man we saw in the saloon tonight. The man you thought was the killer. Fits the description and we heard him called Black and Denny. Plus his initials are DK. Sounds like we got him dead to rights."

Harry spoke again. "This all adds up and if I was the marshal here, I'd say this is enough to lock him up until the traveling judge gets here. But there's one more thing. One thing that makes it real complicated."

Tom asked, "What's that?"

"Denny Kramer is the deputy marshal."

# 9

## FAMILY

THE FOUR MEN stopped talking and simply stared at each other, or the walls, or the window. The realization was now shared and in their minds, it had become indisputable.

Denny Kramer, deputy marshal to Marshal Dan Hoskins of Cheyenne, had beaten two women badly enough they left Cheyenne—though neither left before swearing to Dora that Kramer was the one who beat him.

Following that, things escalated and in less than six months, he had murdered two women as a result of the embarrassment and rage he felt from being unable to 'perform.'

And resting on the nightstand in front of them was the murder weapon, decorated with the killer's initials and sitting among them was a witness to the most recent murder.

Factoring into the decision they had to make was the fact they'd been warned off by the marshal, a man both Huck and Harry believed was hiding the fact that he knew who the killer was but who made no effort to hide his disdain for prostitutes.

Huck broke the silence.

"There's no doubt anymore. There's also no doubt that if something isn't done, he'll kill again. He's gone from slapping around the first girl, to beating the second, to killing the last two. And there is really very doubt little regarding the marshal and the fact he's not going to do anything about this."

Tom asked Huck, "What do you think we should do?"

Harry answered before Huck could. "Huck, a couple of things to think about. One, we've been warned away from getting involved. I might go so far as to say we've been threatened. And you need to be clear that while all of us will do everything we can to protect you and see that justice is carried out, you'll be the target.

"It's also important to remember that we have no friends in this town. Sure, plenty of people will want to see a man like Kramer dealt with, but most won't lift a finger to help. Witnesses have a way of disappearing. I've seen it too many times and can't abide it happening to you."

Huck looked at each of the men before answering, speaking low and slow, "If there was another way to know this man would be dealt with, that these women would be protected and that justice would be served, I'd be happy to saddle up and start out for our new home. But we all know there isn't.

"Harry, Jimmy, we don't know each other well, least not yet. But Tom knows me. We've been through a few things together. He knows I can't leave. No matter what happens, I have to see this through. I'm thinking maybe the best thing is for everyone else to pack up and ride out in the morning.

"When Harry and I were in the marshal's office, he mentioned the circuit judge would be here in three days. I'll wait for him. When it's over, I'll ride out and catch up."

Tom started to speak, but stopped in surprise when Jimmy started to laugh, the first laughter they'd heard all night. When Jimmy stopped laughing, he looked directly at Huck.

"You think I'd want you to run? Leave women to be attacked again? To know what you know and see what you've seen and pretend none of it matters? Son, you're right, we don't know each other well, though we will, maybe startin' now. I wouldn't have my daughter marry anyone who'd do different.

"Only thing is, no one's leavin'. Not me, not Tom, not Harry. Not even my daughter and my Maddie. We'll stay. All of us. We're a family now. We'll stick together through this and if need be, we'll fight together. Come morning, we'll head down to the marshal's office and tell your story.

Maybe he'll do the right thing. Maybe he won't. But we will and we'll wait 'til that circuit judge gets here.

"But we'll do it together, by God. It's the only way."

Huck looked away from Jimmy and saw that Harry and Tom were in full agreement.

"Mr. Huckaby, I appreciate what you said, maybe more than you know. When we get to Montana, you'll meet my father, Brock Clemons. It's exactly what he would have said. And I know Sarah will stay, just like my mother, Sophie, would. Wish I could talk her into leaving, but I know I can't. Guess that's why I fell in love with her.

"Okay, since we're all staying, I have a plan. I'm concerned that maybe with me and Harry at the marshal's office and Harry, now with you visiting Dora, people are going to start noticing. Probably already have. I don't think anything's gonna happen yet, but we can't be too careful. Here's what I'm thinking.

"We move the girls to the last room. Jimmy, you stay in the room with the girls. Means sleeping on the floor, but one of us should be there. Me? I noticed there's a chair at the end of the hall, right next to the window. I'll stay there tonight, watch the hallway. Harry, Tom, you stay in this room. It's closest to the girls. Again, don't really expect anything'll happen tonight, but best to be safe."

Harry added, "It's a good plan. Jimmy, maybe gather up some blankets and just sleep by the door, so no one gets in without waking you up. Huck, you go ahead and take the first shift in the chair, but Tom and I will take turns spellin' ya. In the morning, Huck, you can go back to the marshal's office. Take Tom with you. Jimmy, you stay here with the girls."

Tom asked, "What'll you be doing, Harry?"

"I'm gonna head back to the Bucket o' Beer, let Dora know what we're doing and see if she'll be willing to testify too. Even if she won't, she needs to know what's happening so she can do what she needs to do to protect herself and her girls."

Huck looked around the room and said, "Thank you. Thank you, all."

# 10

## CHARGES

MORNING FOUND everyone safe and sitting around a large round table in the restaurant. No one had slept particularly well, but they'd all gotten some sleep.

They started with milk and coffee, but very little conversation. The coffee tasted good against the morning chill. Winter was fading, but not without a fight. Breakfast was brought to the table and there was plenty of it.

Pancakes, thick and buttered, with a pitcher of maple syrup to be shared. Scrambled eggs and steak, cut thin, which somehow seemed appropriate for breakfast. Biscuits with a thick brown gravy and finally donuts.

Huck had a soft spot for donuts. They brought back memories of his childhood town, Dry Springs, in Colorado Territory and Hattie's, the small restaurant that was owned by Nerissa and her husband, Nolan. Nerissa made the best donuts Huck ever tasted and though he tried them everywhere he went, he'd not found their equal. Not quite eighteen and having never left Dry Springs until he was almost fourteen, Huck had been to many places and seen many things.

He'd lived at the bottom of the Grand Canyon with the Havasupai tribe, where he hoped his friend Kentaki was living safe and happy. He'd lived and worked a silver mine in Cerro Gordo. He'd lived on a small island off the coast of California and he'd driven cattle from Abilene to Montana Territory.

He'd seen men—and women—killed and had been forced to kill men himself. He'd lost his mother when he was born and his father was killed while trying to a break a young horse—the same horse, Spirit, that Huck rides today. He'd lost far too many friends in the past couple of years and it hardened him, while at the same time, it taught him to value family and friends more than many people do.

He'd been adopted by the two best people he knew, Brock and Sophie Clemons. They adopted Annabelle, his younger sister, and later his little brother, Levi, was added to the family. And now, if they could make it through the next few days and then safely travel another six hundred miles across Indian and outlaw infested lands, he was going to marry the prettiest, sweetest girl he'd ever met. Together, they planned to create a life in the ranch and town he and his family and friends were building.

But all of that was behind him (or ahead of him) so he pushed those thoughts aside and did what Brock had taught him—focus on the people you're with and the problem you need to solve. He had plenty to think through and much of what was going to happen was unknown to him—or any of them. What he did know was that these were among the worst donuts he'd ever tasted. He set it down on the plate and instead dished up a healthy helping of biscuits and gravy, covered with a beefsteak.

He realized he hadn't been listening and that Harry had been speaking. He forced himself to focus.

"... all in agreement. Tom and Huck'll head down to the marshal's office. I'll go back to the Bucket and talk to Dora and Jimmy. You'll stay here with Sarah and Maddie."

Tom asked, "So that I'm clear. Huck, you're gonna tell the marshal everything, even though we don't think he's gonna help?

"Yes."

"Even about the knife and Dora?"

"I am. No matter what Harry and I thought about him, we have to give him the chance to do the right thing, or no one will believe us even if this does go to the judge. I know it's a risk, but it's the only way—unless someone else has a different idea."

No one did, so they settled down to do their best to enjoy breakfast.

AN HOUR LATER, Huck and Tom walked into the marshal's office. Hoskins was seated behind his desk, exactly where Harry and Huck had left him. He greeted them with a grunt and pointed to the coffee pot. Tom passed, but Huck poured himself a cup and then they both sat down, though they hadn't been invited to do so.

Hoskins set down his cup, leaned back and said, "Thought I told you it'd be best if you left town?"

"You did."

"So?"

"We didn't agree."

"Don't much care if you agreed or not. This is my town and now I'm tellin' you, it's time for you to leave. Best for everyone if you do and do so right away."

Huck and Tom shared a look, making sure they were still thinking alike. When Huck could tell they were, he continued, "When you say 'everyone,' Marshal, what you really mean is you and your deputy, don't you?"

Hoskins rocked forward and glared at the two, growling, "What the hell you mean?"

"I mean we're here because your deputy, Deputy Kramer, killed Miss Fanny. Stabbed her to death with a twelve-inch Bowie knife and ran like a coward when I saw him."

"You callin' Denny a—"

"A coward. Yes, I am. Any man kills women—"

"Whadda you mean, *women*? You sayin'..."

"I am, Marshal. It is our belief that not only did he kill Miss Fanny, but he killed another woman about six months ago, name of Mollie. Worked at the same place. And before that, he beat two women bad enough they left town."

Hoskins, clearly flustered and angry, started, "How do you...?"

"We know this because we did your job, Marshal. Didn't take much time at all and wasn't too difficult. Talked to a couple of people, asked a few questions, and it fell together quickly. What we have noticed is that you haven't talked to anyone or done anything, which as we understand it, won't surprise many people here in Cheyenne."

"You have no idea who you're talking to or the trouble you're stirring up!"

"I think we have a very good idea, Marshal, on both counts. We're talking to a man who's protecting his deputy, probably because he's afraid of him. We're talking to a man who as much as said he couldn't be bothered to look into the murder of a woman who did what Miss Fanny did to survive.

"Truth is, I don't care much about you. Time has a way of taking care of people like you. What I do care about is the murder, and we're here to file charges against Deputy Denny Kramer for the murder of Miss Fanny."

With that, Huck reached into his pocket, pulled out the

knife and slammed it on the old wooden desk. Hoskins' eyes widened and it was clear he recognized the knife.

Still struggling to take back control of the situation, he blurted, "You think a court'll take your word over my deputy's?"

Before Huck could answer, the front door flew open and a woman Huck and Tom assumed was Dora, stormed in, followed by the smiling former sheriff, Harry Wheeler.

# 11

# NOON

"DORA, WHAT THE HELL..." The marshal was clearly surprised, and not pleasantly, that Dora had walked into his office. "You know you're not supposed to..."

Dora walked, or stomped, until she stood between Huck and Tom. She placed both hands on his big wooden desk and leaned over, staring directly at the flustered marshal.

"I don't care what you think or what arrangement we may have had 'bout me being seen in your office. This has gone too far and you know it."

Trying to regain control, the marshal countered, "I can arrest you right now and you know that."

"Go ahead. You been countin' a long time on me staying quiet 'bout things you don't want people to know. Put me behind bars and watch how fast everyone in this town knows your business. But I ain't here for that. I'm here 'cause your damn deputy killed Miss Fanny and while I don't have any proof, I know he killed Mollie, too."

The marshal tried one more time to bring things back to where he could control them. "Now listen, Dora, without any proof, you got nothing…"

This time it was Harry who spoke up. "Marshal, your deputy is in a world of trouble and you know it. Huck here saw him kill Miss Fanny and Dora will swear in court about the two girls Kramer beat."

"You think the court's gonna listen to a whore?"

Huck, who'd stayed silent until now, stood up, looking far more menacing than most would have thought a seven-teen-year-old could.

"Marshal Hoskins. There's a lot going on here and it seems none of it is good for you or your deputy. I know Kramer killed at least one woman, which is all it'll take for him to hang. And from the sounds of it, Dora may know a couple o' things that could cause you some trouble too. I don't care much about that right now.

"But, if you disrespect this lady one more time, I will reach across that desk and beat you until I run out of strength. You don't know me, but it's best you believe me when I tell you it's not something you want.

"Now, let's talk about what we're gonna do about your deputy." Huck turned toward Dora, saying, "Miss Dora, it is a pleasure to meet you. Please take my seat while we continue our conversation with the marshal here. I believe he should be more willin' to listen politely than he may have been before. Isn't that right, Marshal?"

The marshal, looking dazed and confused and wondering exactly what was happening, simply nodded.

Dora smiled at Huck and took the offered seat, then said, "Now, Marshal, I should have done this a long time ago when your deputy beat two of my girls. But I didn't. And I certainly should have marched down here when he killed Mollie. And don't bother saying anything. We both know he did it.

"But I didn't then either. And for that, I know I can't be forgiven. But I'm here now. Maybe 'cause I've gotten stronger, maybe 'cause Kramer's getting worse, or maybe because these men"—she looked for a moment at Huck, Tom and Harry—"who don't even live in this town have shown the courage to stand up to you and your deputy and I'm ashamed that I haven't.

"Guess it doesn't really matter why, though. What does matter is I'm here now, finally standing up for my girls and ready to file charges against Deputy Marshal Denny 'Black' Kramer."

From behind Dora, Huck added, "I'll be signing those papers, too."

Dora, who hadn't taken her eyes off the marshal, leaned back in her chair, smiled and asked, "So whadda you going to do now"—and she spat out the last word—"*Marshal*?"

"Well, the judge is gonna be here soon."

"We know that, but it's not good enough. You need to lock him up now. If you don't, you know he's gonna be comin' after all of us, startin' with me and Huck here."

The marshal, who now looked scared, answered, "Dora, you know Black. You know what he'll do if I try to arrest him."

Dora didn't back down. "Marshal, that's your problem now, isn't it? You've let him do anything he wants to anyone he wants for a long time. Long as no one complained too loudly—and you got your cut—you were happy to let him have his way. Well, Dan, the time has come. Payment's due. This is your problem now and you better figure it out."

Before the marshal could answer, though he didn't have a good one, Harry spoke up.

"Marshal, it's ten o'clock. We'll give you 'til noon to lock Kramer up and then hold him until the judge arrives. Once you lock him up, we'll even help you guard him, though it doesn't sound like he's got a lotta friends that'll be comin' to help. But it's your job to put him behind bars."

"And if I don't?"

"Then we'll do it for you. Thing is, we'll be putting you in the same cell as Kramer. Can't promise that'll go well for you but even if it does, based on what Miss Dora's been tellin' me, there's plenty to get you sent away. You been doing this long enough to know ex-marshals don't do real well in prison."

Desperate, the marshal croaked, "Isn't there anything..."

Dora answered, "Marshal, too many deals been cut for too long and not just with me. You don't have many friends here in town, and you've been hidin' behind Black for too long. Now, I got no need to press charges against you—as long as Black stands trial for murder. That's as close to a deal as you're gonna get. I suggest you take it."

Without waiting for an answer, Dora stood up, with Huck pulling out her chair. Tom, who hadn't said a word but had watched in amazement, stood as well and joined the other three as they headed for the door.

Harry, who had held the door open for Dora, Huck and Tom, looked back at the marshal as he stepped out, and said, "Noon, Marshal. Twelve o'clock."

# 12

# DEATH

THE FOUR OF them left the marshal's office and walked down the boardwalk. The hotel, restaurant and bar were only a few doors down and they headed in that direction. When Huck looked inside, he saw that Jimmy, Maddie and Sarah were still sitting at the table. The breakfast plates were cleared away, but they were all enjoying a cup of coffee.

Jimmy had his back to the wall and was positioned so he could watch the front door and was the first to see the four. Huck started to open the door when Dora pulled back, obviously uncomfortable and nervous. He looked at her as he held the door and said, "Please join us for a cup of coffee. There are people I'd like you to meet."

She hesitated before saying, "Huck, this is very sweet,

but I don't think I'd be welcome at the Shy Anne. Never been inside, and I think they prefer it that way."

"They might, but we don't. Now, please join us for a cup of coffee. It won't take long."

She reluctantly agreed and was about halfway to the table when the owner, John McCarthy, saw her and walked over, looking angry. As he approached, he said, "Miss Dora, you shouldn't—"

This time it was Tom who stepped forward. "You are speaking to a friend of ours, so allow me to finish your sentence for you, since I think I can guess what you were going to say.

"Miss Dora, you shouldn't have taken so long to visit us. Welcome to the Shy Anne."

McCarthy looked around the restaurant and then back at the four and finally, directly at Dora. With a sigh of acceptance, he said, "Yes, that's exactly what I was going to say. Allow me to bring another chair so that there is room for everyone."

With that, everyone relaxed, introductions were made and coffee was served, along with some biscuits and donuts. Everyone was brought up to date with the morning's activities and wondered what would happen between then and noon. When they were done talking, they paid their bill, and Dora graciously accepted what seemed like a heartfelt apology from Mr. McCarthy.

Huck and Tom agreed to walk Dora back to the Bucket o'
Beer and Jimmy and Harry walked the girls upstairs, wanting
to make sure they were safe. Huck, Tom and Dora started
back down the boardwalk since the Bucket o' Beer was on
the opposite side of the marshal's office from the restaurant.
They ignored the stares from those who were out and about.

When they were about fifty feet past the marshal's
office, the door opened. With the noise from the shops and
horses on the dusty street, they didn't hear it. Dora
happened to turn around, thinking someone had called out
to her and instead saw Black racing toward them, his face
pulled back in an evil grin and his right hand raised above
his head and holding his Bowie knife, which he'd obviously been given by, or taken from, the marshal.

He was fewer than ten feet away from Huck, obviously
his intended target, and was screaming, though no one
could understand what he was saying. Huck whirled when
Dora yelled. As he saw Black barreling down on him, he
dropped his hand to Remington 1858 and with a speed and
smoothness honed over thousands of practice rounds, he
drew and shot Black three times in the chest. He was dead
before he hit the ground, his knife tumbling harmlessly off
the boardwalk and onto the street.

Following not too far behind Black was Marshal
Hoskins, his gun already drawn. He pointed it at Huck and
a little more loudly and shrilly than he would have liked,
yelled at Huck, "Drop your gun! I saw the whole thing.

You shot an unarmed man. My deputy, which makes it worse. I'm bringing you in until Judge Strawbridge gets here."

Tom and Dora started to protest, but Hoskins cut them off. "Nothing you two can say's gonna matter. No one's gonna listen to a drifter or a whore."

So fast no one saw it coming, especially the marshal, who was staring at Dora, Huck exploded and knocked the marshal to the ground. His gun slipped from his hand before he could use it to try and stop Huck. Huck was pummeling him when Tom and another man were finally able to pull him off.

The marshal's face was bloody and he was slow trying to get up. Huck looked at him, his chest heaving, and said, "I told you what would happen if you disrespected her again."

The marshal, who'd managed to pick up his gun, finally stood up and looked at Huck, saying, "You'll go away for this. This and killing a deputy."

The man who helped Tom pull Huck away spoke for the first time and also for the first time, the marshal noticed who he was. The man said, "Marshal, I saw the whole thing from across the street. Deputy Kramer would have killed this man if he'd been any slower. It was self-defense and if you make me do so by arresting this man, I'll testify to that."

"Reverend?"

"Like I said, Don, self-defense, and Judge Strawbridge will believe me. I think you know that."

"Reverend. You'd testify against me? In favor of these drifters?"

"Marshal, I testify to the truth. No matter who. No matter what."

Before the marshal could respond, Dora spoke.

"Marshal, you should know I've decided to testify as well. And I mean about *everything*. How you and Black stole money from the townspeople. How you never prosecuted your friends but went after anyone you considered an enemy. And I'll testify that you knew what Black had done to my girls and kept quiet 'cause you were afraid of Black and how they were only—"

The marshal snapped. Everything he'd worked for was crashing down on top of him. He knew if Dora testified, he'd be going to prison. He got a crazed look on his face, very much like the one Black had when he attacked Huck. He turned toward Dora, raising his gun and his voice as he did, shouting, "You'll never...!"

Before he could finish, Tom pulled his gun and shot the marshal dead. He crashed to the boardwalk, his gun following Black's knife onto the dusty street.

# 13

# STRAW

TWO DAYS LATER, the six travelers were enjoying their mid-day meal at the Shy Anne Hotel and Eatery. They were joined by Dora, whose last name they had learned was Rossi, and the reverend, whose full name was Mike Periwinkle, an unusual last name that none of them had heard before.

In the short time since they'd killed Black and the marshal, things had changed in Cheyenne. Dora was now welcome inside the Shy Anne. Everyone learned she had been forced to pay the marshal for protection—from everyone except Black. Harry had been offered the job of town marshal, which he quickly and politely turned down.

None of the eight had been allowed to pay for a meal or a drink since the shootings. Though both Huck and Tom felt a little awkward being rewarded for killing a man, they understood how the town felt.

Both had thought back to when they were thirteen and their town, Dry Springs, was rapidly falling under the control of a cruel outlaw named Kurt and the equally cruel men who worked for him. They had killed a couple of the men in town and those who remained were scared. No one knew how many more men would have died or what would have happened to the town, but that all changed when Brock Clemons rode into town.

Brock had rallied the townsfolk and showed them that they could fight their own battles, though he still led the way and wound up killing Kurt and most of the gang. He also fell in love with Sophie, married her and adopted Huck. The three of them left for a two-week trip to adopt Brock's sister, who had been left orphaned when Brock's father was killed.

They wound up never returning, except for a couple of quick visits. Life had been one continuous adventure from the moment they rode out of town. About a year previously, Tom joined Huck and they'd been traveling together ever since.

It was hard for Huck to remember anything else and he had to remind himself that this was all new to Sarah, as it had once been to him. She'd met hard men in Abilene, but never had to live through anything like what they'd all been through over the past few days.

At first Huck worried that she might be scared off. That she might change her mind about marrying him and moving to Montana Territory. But she hadn't faltered. They hadn't slept much the past two nights as they sat up both nights while Huck finally shared with her some of the other things he had been through since leaving Dry Springs.

While it gave her a different perspective on what life might be like where they were headed, she seemed to embrace it, or at least understand it. Huck was a little surprised, but relieved at the same time. He was certain that Jimmy was going through something similar with Maddie, but she also seemed quite willing to face the challenges that lay ahead.

Dora was in the middle of telling a story about being raised in New York City, a place none of them had been to, when the front door was thrown open by a man who couldn't be any taller than five foot four and couldn't weigh more than a hundred and twenty pounds. He had on an expensive leather coat and boots that looked like they'd just been shined. He wore a bright blue shirt and a hat, really more of a beanie, and it had a single white feather sticking out the back.

Before the door closed, John McCarthy yelled across the restaurant, "Judge Straw! How are you?"

"I'm good, Mac. How 'bout you?"

"Been a while since I've been this good, Judge. Things have changed since you were last here."

"I guess they have. I've only been here twenty minutes and all I've been hearing about is what happened to Black and the marshal. Most folks seem to think they had it coming."

"Won't get an argument from me, Judge. Allow me to introduce you to the men, and woman, responsible."

McCarthy walked the judge over to where the two tables were pushed together. With a sense of pride, he started the introductions. "Judge, this is Jimmy Huckaby and his fiancée, Maddie Saw..."

Harry jumped in and saved him. "Stawarski. It's Stawarski, Mac."

"Thanks, Harry. Can't quite get that to roll off my tongue. My apologies, ma'am. Anyway, sitting next to him is Harry Wheeler, a former sheriff from down in Abilene. Next to him is Tom James. He's the one shot Marshal Hoskins. Next to him is Reverend Mike Periwinkle, though I believe you already know the reverend. Huck Clemons, who killed Black, is next to him, and next to him is his fiancée—also Mr. Huckaby's daughter, the beautiful Sarah. And next to her—"

"Next to her is the equally beautiful Dora Rossi. Miss Dora and I are acquainted." He tipped his hat toward each of them, lingering on Dora. "If none of you mind, I'll ask our kind owner to bring an extra chair and an extra plate.

I've come a long way and I'm hungry. I also understand you good people have a story to tell me."

Huck watched as Dora gently patted the judge on the thigh and then figured he might as well be the one to tell the story. The judge asked a question or two as Huck told what happened. It took about a half hour and he finished the story about the same time as the judge finished eating.

The judge looked up at McCarthy, who'd remained standing the entire time. "Mac, that what happened?"

"Wasn't there, Judge, but that's exactly how I've heard it from those who were."

"Reverend?"

"I can't speak to the parts before the shooting, but I was there for both shootings and that's how they happened."

"Miss Dora?"

"I wouldn't change a word, Judge, and I'd sign any paper needs signing."

The judge took the last large bite of a pork chop and when he was done chewing, he looked around the table at each of them and then up at McCarthy.

"John, you still make the best chops in the Territory. Worth the coach ride over just for these. As for the rest of you, case closed. Been thinking for a while those two men weren't dealing fair, but I didn't know exactly what to do about it. As for your story, if the reverend and Miss Dora say that's how it happened, then by God, that's how it happened.

"Now, John, bring us a couple of your pies and bring me the check for the whole meal."

Jimmy was the first one who tried to stop the judge, but he was waved off by the smaller man. "After what you did for this town, it's the least we can do. Anyway, I'll charge it back to the marshal's office once they find a new marshal."

When everyone was done laughing and the pies had been sliced up and shared, the judge patted the corners of his mouth with this napkin, took a sip of the whiskey that seemed to appear from nowhere and said, "Now, maybe you good folks can tell me where you're from, where you're going and what you plan on doing when you get there. I love a good story."

# 14

# CASPER

IT WAS A LITTLE OVER A WEEK, a pleasantly uneventful week, when the six rolled into Casper. The trip from Cheyenne to Casper was a few miles short of two hundred, but without running into bad people or bad weather, it was as easy a trip as could be hoped for. It was only an hour past dawn when they arrived and it was still cold enough to make a hot cup of coffee a top priority. Huck had insisted they camp just outside of town the night before, having learned from Brock it's always a better idea to enter a new town in light of day.

Though he and Tom had stopped briefly in Casper on their way from their new home to Abilene to pick up Sarah, Huck's mind went back to the first time he'd been here.

He'd ridden into town after driving two thousand head

of cattle seven hundred miles from Abilene. Actually, it was Gus Seldon and the dozen men he'd brought with him who'd driven the cattle. Huck, Tom, and his two Havasupai friends, Kentaki and Tochopa, learned as they went, but in no way would they be considered cattlemen, at least not then.

That trip from Abilene had been full of adventure and challenges, including severe weather and having to kill ten cattle rustlers, but their group and all the cattle arrived safely.

Huck had been shocked to find that his family had arrived in Casper the same time as he had. They had left Santa Cruz Island, off the coast of California, where they had been managing the island's sheep for a man named Gustave Mahe. Mr. Mahe had convinced them to move to Montana Territory and partner with him in starting a large cattle ranch. The partnership was simple. He would provide the money for the land and cattle and Brock, Sophie and whoever they hired would do all the work.

On their way from California to Montana Territory, they had stopped in Dry Springs and then made their way to Casper, arriving at the same time as Huck and the cattle. The happy and surprising reunion was temporarily cut short when Huck was arrested for nearly beating a man to death who had insulted and threatened his mother. That was resolved and everyone eventually made it safely to their new home, something Huck hoped was going to happen again this time—without the arrest and near hanging.

With everything that happened in Cheyenne, they had completely forgotten to have the wagon looked at and any necessary repairs made while they were there. The trails are hard on wagons and they were fortunate the lack of upkeep hadn't caused them trouble on this most recent leg of the trip. Not wanting to press their luck, they went straight to the livery and made arrangements for the wagon to be taken care of, as well as the horses.

When that was done, Tom turned to Huck and said, "Remember where we stayed the first time, the Fort Caspar Grub? Jimmy, I think his name was. They have those rooms upstairs he rents out sometimes. Bet he'll let us stay here for a night or two if we want to rest up before the final push. Also remember him having a pretty good breakfast and some fine coffee."

Huck could tell that everyone thought this was an excellent idea, so they started the short walk from the livery to the Grub. On the way, they passed the Casper General Store, the exact spot where Huck had been so surprised to find his mother and sister last year. Sadness swept over Huck as he remembered learning that Reverend Matt Lavender, one of the two or three men Huck admired most in his life, had been killed on the trail.

Knowing how often death found those who spent any length of time on the trails didn't make it any easier. It still hurt Huck when he thought about it. It was made even worse when Matt's wife, Stacy, couldn't take it anymore and simply left on a train one morning. The destination was unknown, no note had been left, but everyone understood. Her leaving was hardest on his mother, Sophie, who somehow felt responsible for Matt's death.

Huck tried to shake off the sadness as they all walked into the Fort Caspar Grub. He remembered that the spelling was different than that of the town out of respect to the man the town was named after, Lieutenant Caspar, who was killed in the Battle of the Red Buttes. The owner of the Fort Caspar Grub, Jimmy, was then known as Corporal James Williams, one of only three men who survived the battle, or as he described it, the massacre.

And that's the man who greeted the six as they walked in. It took him a moment to remember Huck and Tom, but he soon did and seemed genuinely glad to see them.

After introductions were made and in answer to Tom's question, Jimmy answered, "Of course, you can stay here. How many rooms?"

Told they needed three, Jimmy said, "Let's get some breakfast started for you and then I'll make sure the rooms are clean and ready. For now, you can just set your cases over in the corner."

Huck looked over to the corner Jimmy was pointing at

and saw a familiar face, Sheriff Ken Clark. The sheriff was staring back at Huck and Tom and clearly recognized them. Huck turned to everyone and said, "Give me a minute. I need to speak to the sheriff over there."

Tom offered, "You want I should go with you?"

"No. Thanks, Tom, but I'd best go alone." He walked across the small restaurant and when he reached the table where the sheriff was sitting alone, nursing a cup of coffee, he reached out his hand. The sheriff took it and Huck started, "Sheriff, my name's—"

"Son, I know who you are. Huck Clemons, right?"

"Yessir."

"And the one with you, one who tried to break you out of my jail, that'd be..."

"Tom James, sir. A friend of mine, as you know."

"And the others?"

"Well, sir, I'd be happy to introduce you to all of them. Even have you join us, if you'd like. Guess I just wanted to be sure..."

"Wanted to be sure you're still welcome here, after what happened?"

"Yes. I guess so, sir."

"Son, a couple a things. First, quite callin' me sir. Makes me feel old. As far as what happened, we settled that back then. Cactus Bill was a fool to threaten your mother and though you may have gone too far with the beatin', pretty sure I woulda done the same if it'd been my mother.

Anyway, don't matter now and you and yours are welcome here. And yes."

"Yes?"

"Yes, I'd like to meet your people and join you for another cup of coffee."

# 15

## ENYETO

THEY HAD A NICE BREAKFAST. After helping to prepare the eggs, rolls, pancakes and fruit, Jimmy Williams sat and joined them. He and the sheriff shared that not much had happened in town since Huck's trouble and they both promised to try and visit the new ranch.

They'd heard good things about the area and were especially intrigued about maybe seeing Yellowstone National Park, which was not only the nation's first national park, but the first one anywhere in the world. It had only been the previous year when President Ulysses S. Grant signed the National Park Protection Act that created the park. They'd read about the 'geysers' but had never seen onc and had a little trouble believing they were real.

They were all discussing possible times for the men to visit when once again Huck was shocked to see a familiar face. This time it was Maria Hinojosa. Maria, along with her husband Cisco, her son, Enyeto, her sister Catalina and her husband Alex 'Clybs' Clyburn had followed Brock up from Tesuque, a tiny little town north of Santa Fe in the Territory of New Mexico.

Brock had been searching for his father, the reason he moved to America from London. While he hadn't found him, at least not then, he had saved the lives of all those people and they accepted his invitation to move to Dry Springs. It became a pattern in Brock's life that people he would meet in his travels would follow him to wherever he was headed. Huck always admired how much people trusted his father enough to uproot their lives and move to places they'd never been, to chase dreams they might not have even known they'd had.

Maria had been a part of his life for the past few years and he loved her as he imagined one would an aunt. She was his mother's best friend and Huck couldn't understand why she was in Casper. But for now, he stood up, yelled her name and raced across the restaurant floor, meeting her at the bottom of the stairs.

She fell into his arms and within moments was sobbing. He held her closely, while Tom, who had followed Huck over, having known her as long as Huck had, watched with concern.

After a couple of minutes, Huck gently pushed Maria

back and asked her, "Maria, what are you... how are you... who else..."

Without stopping her crying, she blurted out, "Huck, it's been terrible."

"What? What's wrong, Maria? What's happened? Is Cisco okay?"

"He is, but he's hurt. His leg. But Enyeto..."

She couldn't finish the sentence, leaving Huck and Tom to guess what happened. Neither of them could come up with a good answer. Huck and Tom half carried, half held Maria as they guided her to the table. A chair was quickly added and she slumped down into it. Though neither of them had ever met Maria, both Sarah and Maddie were up instantly from their chairs and each of them kneeled by her side. They didn't say a word, they just held her.

The table was silent as Maria slowly pulled herself together. Jimmy eventually whispered to Huck, though others could hear him, "She and her husband rode into town a little over a week ago. She's been staying here ever since. Her husband's leg was badly hurt and he hasn't been downstairs since me and Doc carried him up. Doc checks on him most days. I don't know who Enyeto is and I didn't know she knew you. She only said she was from up north. She comes down maybe once a day. I prepare a basket of food and she takes it back up."

Huck answered, "Enyeto is her son. Her first husband, P'oe, was Cisco's best friend and when he was killed by outlaws, Cisco married her and has been raising Enyeto as his own. My father, Brock, saved Cisco from the same outlaws that killed P'oe and they have been friends ever since. I don't understand why they're here. They were living on the ranch with my family. They are family."

Just then, Maria, her sobbing down to a whimper, looked up at Huck and spoke in a voice so low they could barely hear it.

"My Enyeto, he was killed. He and Cisco... they were... they were riding a horse on our way here and they were galloping. Enyeto, he was laughing so hard. The horse, it tripped and when it fell, Enyeto was killed and Cisco's leg was shattered. It was horrible. Little Enyeto, his neck..."

Huck couldn't help but think back to when he watched his father's neck broken in a riding accident. The image never left Huck, neither had the sense of loss. Maria continued.

"I buried my son. He is alongside the trail between here and the new ranch. Once I could get Cisco in the wagon, we came here. The doctor said Cisco will live, but walking will be hard. We have stayed here while he tried to get stronger, so we can keep going back home."

Huck reached out and set his hand on her arm, saying, "Maria, I am so sorry. I loved Enyeto like a little brother. He was a good boy. And Cisco, I will go see him, but first, why were you alone on the trail? Did something happen at the ranch?"

"No. Nothing happened. Everyone is safe there, or they were when we left. Your father killed the terrible man and that danger has passed. But the winter. It was hard and we did not like it. Me and Cisco, we missed our home. We missed Tesuque and we missed our families. We decided to leave and go back home. We were going to go to Dry Springs first and try to talk Cat and Alex to come with us and we could all start over there. But then..."

She started sobbing again and was quickly cradled by Sarah and Maddie. Huck looked to the sheriff, who stood up and waved Huck away from the table. When they were out of earshot of the others, he started.

"Doc said his leg is terrible. He might be able to travel but he would be of no help on the trip. It would be hard. This Maria, she may be a strong woman, buy she cannot think it would be wise for the two of them to try and travel more than six hundred miles. That is a hard enough trip for healthy men, but one woman, with an injured man, it would not work."

"Did Doc really say he would recover?"

"Yes. His leg will never be the same, but unless something else happens, he should recover. It is just that it will be months. Huck, there is one more thing the Doc told me that you should know."

"Yes?"

"Your friend, she is with child."

# 16

## CISCO

THIS TIME it was Huck who needed to take a seat. The loss of Enyeto, the injury to Cisco and now this. He looked up and asked the sheriff, "How far along is she? Do you know?"

"Doc says about halfway."

Huck looked over at the table where the girls were still consoling Maria. The others were sitting around wordlessly, having no idea what to say or do. Huck knew he needed to figure something out, that they couldn't abandon their friends. His thoughts drifted to his father and he wondered what he would do. After a moment, the answer came to him. He looked over at the table and waved Tom toward him and the sheriff. A few steps and he was there.

"Tom, let's go upstairs and talk to Cisco. Sheriff, let them know we'll be back in a bit, will ya?"

"Of course."

As they walked up the stairs, Tom asked Huck, "Whadda we gonna do?"

"I got an idea." And with that he knocked on the door of room number three and heard a fairly weak voice say, "Come in."

Tom and Huck opened the door and saw Cisco lying in one of the two beds that were in the darkened room. It took a moment for Cisco to recognize them and when he did, he called out, "Huck. Tom. How did you know? Where's Maria?"

The two approached the bed with Tom opening the drapes and letting some sunlight into the room, before taking the one chair and Huck sitting on the bed's edge. "Maria's fine. Or I guess as fine as she can be. She's downstairs with everyone else and they're looking after her. We didn't know, Cisco. We didn't have any idea.

"We're just riding through on our way to the ranch, heading back from Abilene. We were having breakfast when Maria came down the stairs. She started to tell us what happened, but she couldn't continue."

The tears came quickly to Cisco's eyes and he took a moment to gather himself before replying.

"It was me. I killed Enyeto. He loved riding fast. Maria always said it was dangerous, but he loved it so much. He was very hard to say no to. You know that smile he had."

Huck and Tom both nodded with the memory of the little boy everyone loved.

"He sat in front of me, like he always did, and we went for a little ride. We never let Maria and wagon out of our sight. Enyeto screamed with joy and yelled, 'Faster! Faster!' I could never go fast enough for him. He had no fear.

"It was a beautiful day. The sun was out. It was the first day we didn't need our heavy coats. Most of the snow had melted away. There was a light breeze. We had stopped for our mid-day meal and while Maria was preparing it, I thought a short ride would be fun.

"We saw some antelope off in the distance, so we took off after them. We weren't even hunting, just riding. I never saw the hole and the horse's front leg stepped right into it. Shattered right away. Enyeto was thrown clear, but he must have broken his neck when he landed. I tumbled over the front of the horse and then it landed on my left leg. I couldn't move. I couldn't get to my son.

"Maria came running. It must have been a half mile. She was crying before she got to us. She went to Enyeto first, and I could tell he was dead by the way she reacted. She tried to move the horse, but she couldn't. I had to shoot it while she went back and got the wagon and the second horse. She tied the dead horse to the good one and she was able to move it enough to free my leg.

"It was two days before I could move at all. Maria had to bury her son without me helping. Huck, Tom, she had to dig her baby's grave. That hurt so much more than the leg. Eventually, I was able to crawl and between us, I got into the wagon. Maria got us here, but by then I had blacked out. When I woke up, I was in this room.

"Doc says in a few months, my leg will heal, least as well as it's ever going to. He says I'll be able to walk, but I'll need a cane. But not for a few months. I don't know what to do. We don't have enough money to live like this, to live here, for a few months. And there's something else."

Huck looked at Tom first, then at Cisco and said, "Maria's going to have a baby."

Cisco started, "How did you..."

"The sheriff told me. Doc told him. Cisco, is that why you left the ranch?"

"Yes, mostly. Maria wanted to be with her sister, with her family when she had this baby, our baby. No, she didn't like the winter, but mostly it was her sister. It bothered her much more than it bothered me, but I couldn't tell her no. She's been through so much and has asked for so little."

"Cisco, did Cat know she was coming? That you were on your way to Dry Springs?"

"I think so. Maria sent her and Clybs a letter when we went through Bozeman. It's probably there by now."

"Okay. We'll send her a letter from here. I'll write it and we'll post it tomorrow. The thing is Cisco, I'm going to tell her you're not coming."

"You're what? You can't do that. Maria—"

"Cisco, you and I both know you can't make the trip to Dry Springs and certainly not all the way to Tesuque. Not with your leg and not with Maria, well, you know."

"Then what can we do?"

"You'll come with us, back to the ranch. We'll nurse your leg back to health and take care of Maria until she has the baby. Come next spring, if you still want to go back home, of course you can go then. In my letter, I'll ask Cat and Clybs to come and live on the ranch, even if it's just 'til you leave again. If they move fast, they can be there before the baby."

Cisco, with more tears in his eyes, said, "I can't ask you to do that, Huck. It's too much."

Before Huck could answer, Tom did. "Cisco, if it was Brock lying here, right where you are, and Sophie was downstairs in the kind of pain Maria is in, what would you do?"

Cisco answered, "Anything I could to help."

Tom continued, "And why?"

"Because they are like family..."

The three men smiled at the same time. Huck said, "I'll check with the doc and see how soon we can leave."

# 17

# CAT

THE FOLLOWING morning found everyone on the second floor of the small hotel, crammed into room number three. Cisco whispered to Huck that it was the first time he'd seen Maria smile since the accident.

Maddie had the chair, everyone else was spread between the two beds, except Huck, who stood by the window, where he said, "Doc's not thrilled about it, but says if we have to, we can start out in three days."

Cisco started to object. "You can't wait another three days. I know you need to get back to the ranch. Maria and me will catch up when we can, promise."

Huck laughed and answered, "Sarah, Maddie, we leaving here without Maria?"

Cisco, who didn't know either woman, knew enough

about women to understand their reaction made it perfectly clear that they'd all be leaving together.

"Okay, thank you. Truth is, I don't know what we woulda done and if we coulda made it without you. Don't know how we can ever repay you."

Huck laughed again. "Cisco, we've ridden enough trails together and saved each other often enough, ain't no one keepin' a ledger. People are nice here anyway and after the time we had in Cheyenne, another couple of days isn't gonna matter. Now, I wrote that letter to Cat. You want to read it and see if it says what you want?"

Huck watched as a look was exchanged between Cisco and Maria. Cisco answered, "Huck, we can't read English. You write it in Spanish, we'll read it, but not in English. Never learned."

Sarah spoke next. "Maria? Cisco? How 'bout I read the letter to you and you see if you want any changes?"

They both nodded and Sarah took the letter from Huck and started reading.

*Cat,*

*You should know this letter is from me, Huck Clemons, not your sister or Cisco. It's a hard letter to write and there's some bad news in it. By now, you've maybe received a letter from Maria, telling you they're coming to see you and hoping you'll leave Dry Springs and move back to Tesuque with them.*

*Things have happened since she wrote that and some of it is horrible. There's no easy way to say this, so I'm just come out* with it. Little Enyeto was killed in a terrible accident. He was riding with Cisco and the horse spilled. He died fast. Wish I didn't have to tell you.

Cisco was hurt too. He'll be okay, but not for a while. Shattered his leg pretty bad. Doc said worse he's seen, but not many. Means they can't get to Dry Springs. It's too far for them to make the trip alone, especially since Cisco won't be able to do much, least for a while.

Cat, there's another thing and this one is good news. Your sister is gonna have a baby. She's been with the doc here and he says she's plenty healthy and maybe halfway along. All this means their plans have changed, have had to change.

We're in Casper now. That's in Wyoming Territory. Almost five hundred miles from our ranch in Yellowstone. They're going to come back home with us. We'll be there in plenty of time for the baby and it'll let Cisco's leg get better without him having to work too hard.

We're all hoping you and Clybs will leave Dry Springs and head up there. The ranch has plenty of room and Maria wants to have her sister with her. They'll stay through the winter and then decide next spring if they still want to go back to Tesuque. You can stay too.

I think you'd like it. It's even prettier than Dry Springs. We've started a ranch and have two thousand head of cattle. The main ranch house is built, so is the main bunkhouse. And so is my house, where my soon-to-be wife, Sarah, and I will live. Tom James is still with us (please tell his folks he's doing well) *and he'd kill me for telling you this, but he's fallen for a local girl.*

At this point Tom interrupted, "You can't put that in a letter!"

Huck laughed. "Too late, it's already written, plus it's true and anyone who's seen you around her knows it." Huck relished his friend's embarrassment for a moment and then Sarah kept reading.

*Cat, I know this is a lot in one letter and I wish I had better news for you. But if you leave right away, you can be to the ranch before the baby. Maria wants me to tell you she loves you and hopes you will come. As soon as you receive this and decide, please send a letter to Maria in Bozeman, in Montana Territory. We check the mail there often.*

*With great hope,*

*Huck*

When Sarah finished reading, Cisco and Maria looked at each other, gave slight smiles and nodded. They took a pencil from the nightstand and each signed the letter.

Huck handed Sarah the envelope on which he'd already written Cat's Dry Springs address. She folded the letter neatly and slid it inside.

Huck took it back, saying as he did, "I'm gonna walk this over to the post office right now. If I remember right, it's inside of the Casper General Store. While I'm there, I'll check and see if any of us got any mail."

Huck walked out, leaving his friends and family to

catch up with each other, hoping the conversation would ease Cisco and Maria's pain, all the while knowing it would never fully go away. Once again, he thought of his father and wondered what life might have been like if he hadn't been killed. He thought maybe he'd have wound up working at the livery his father owned, maybe for most of his life. Marry a local girl and have a couple of children.

There was a time when that might have been enough. But now, Huck had been too many places and seen too many things to ever imagine living that life. As they were beginning to draw closer to Yellowstone, he began to wonder what his life was going to look like.

He'd been so focused on setting up the ranch and marrying Sarah, he hadn't put much thought at all into what would happen next.

## 18

# BOXED X

It was a short walk to the Casper General Store. Huck enjoyed the few minutes to himself. The weather was crisp and while you could wear a coat and not get overly warm, you could also comfortably wear just a shirt, which was what Huck chose to do, leaving his coat at the hotel.

There were a few clouds drifting by in the light breeze, which only made the brilliant blue of the sky stand out even more. There were a handful of people on the boardwalk, shopkeepers getting ready for the day, men going to work, women starting their shopping. Everyone seemed relaxed and Huck enjoyed the feeling of relative safety, knowing all too well how infrequent that was.

He stepped into the general store, noticing three other men shopping and one man behind the counter. He walked up to the counter and introduced himself and was greeted with a warm smile and an outreached hand.

"Name's Troy. What can I help you with?"

"I'd like to post this letter. It's heading to Colorado Territory."

"Pretty good timing, I'd say. Mail leaves here weekly and it's scheduled for this afternoon."

"Thank you. It's important that it get there as soon as possible, so this is very good news. As long as I'm here, let me check to see if we've got any mail waiting for us." Huck gave the clerk the name of everyone in their party and ended with, "... and I'm Huck Clemons, so any for me or anyone else at the Circle CM."

The clerk excused himself and headed toward the back, where he kept the stack of letters that built up over time. As he did, the three men in the store approached Huck. All three were dressed like they'd spent some time on the trail and they all looked like they could handle themselves. Huck wasn't expecting any trouble in Casper, but he knew it paid to be cautious.

He turned to face the three men, his right hand sliding down close to his holster, saying, "Good morning, gentlemen. Something I can help you with, or are you waiting for the clerk to come back?"

The smallest of three spoke first. "No, wanting to talk to you. Heard you say the Circle CM?"

Huck's shoulders tensed and he looked at each of the

three men. He didn't see any aggression but remained cautious. "I did. It's my family's ranch. Take it you heard of it?"

"Yessir, we have. We ride with the Boxed Y."

"Sorry, boys. I'm fairly new to the territory and I haven't heard of the Boxed Y. You from around here?"

"We're not. We're from up your way. Our ranch used to be known as the Boxed X."

As soon as Huck heard that, he started to reach for his gun. As he drew it, all three men raised their hands and smiled, just about the last thing Huck expected.

The small man spoke again. "Slow down there, Huck. It is Huck, right?"

"It is. And you did say the Boxed X, right?"

"I did, but to be clear, I said it *used* to be known as the Boxed X. Guess you haven't heard what happened. Now that I think about it, I remember hearing about another Clemons, one who was headin' down to Abilene to meet a girl."

"That's me. Huck Clemons. By another Clemons, I'm guessing you're familiar with my mother and father, Sophie and Brock? Sounds like you know a little about me, but I don't know anything about you and what I know about the X ain't good. You might think me unfriendly, but until I know more, how 'bout you keep your hands where I can see 'em."

One of the other men started to speak. He had a

friendly smile on his face as he did. "Since you haven't heard, we can understand you being less than friendly. I promise you, we're not looking for any trouble. If you let us buy you a cup of coffee, I think you'll find what we have to say to be good news."

The clerk walked out of the back room, holding a single letter in his hand. He stopped cold when he saw the drawn gun. He started to turn around when Huck said, "Sorry, Troy. Looks like this might have been a misunderstanding. These men are about to explain why." Looking at the letter in the clerk's hand, Huck continued, "Is that for me?"

"Yessir, it is."

Huck holstered his gun, took the letter without looking at it and shoved it in his back pocket. "I'm not traveling alone and everyone else is back at the hotel. How about we head back there for that cup of coffee?"

"Okay with us. Invite all of them to join if you like. We're buying."

The four left together and a few minutes later they were seated around two tables shoved together, along with Tom, Jimmy and Harry. The girls stayed with Cisco and Maria in the room.

Introductions were made and the Circle CM men learned that the smaller man was named Hank Thompson and the other two were Leo Watkins and Timothy Abernathy. When the coffee had been served, Hank started up the conversation.

"First, sorry if we startled you back there. Didn't mean to. I know there was bad blood between the X and your ranch. Can't say we didn't have at least something to do with that. But things have changed since you rode out and I guess we should have thought about that."

Huck, still not completely relaxed, asked, "Changed how? Changing the name doesn't seem like it would fix the problem."

"Normally, you're right. But not this time. Clint Beck and nine of us..."

Huck's mind drifted to Beck and the fact he hated the Circle CM, Brock, and most of all his mother, Sophie. Beck was greedy and mean and couldn't accept a woman running a ranch, which Sophie did. He especially hated it when that ranch was bigger than his beloved Boxed X, which the Circle CM was.

Clint and his men had tried on more than one occasion to kill Brock and some of the others but had been stopped every time. Huck didn't know if these three had been involved in any of the attempts, but he was having trouble seeing how this breakfast was going to turn out well.

# 19

# BOXED Y

HANK CONTINUED, "...rode up to your ranch. Clint was sure he could scare everyone off this time and if that didn't work, he was gonna kill your father and anyone else he thought stood in his way.

"Some of us started to think the old man was losing it, but it turns out he'd already lost it. Like I said, we rode up to the ranch, Clint out front. Brock met us, stood alone against the ten of us. The man has sand, I'll give 'em that. Not the first time he'd stood up to the Boxed X, or against Clint. Clint wasn't used to having anyone stand up to him. 'Til your father showed up, not sure anyone had in years, maybe ever.

"Well, when we got there, Clint ordered us to kill everyone on the ranch, including women and children."

It took everything Huck had to not leap over the table

at the three men, but he restrained himself, though not without a struggle.

"Now we ride for the brand like we all do. Like you do. Things had been sliding for a while, but most of us don't know when to quit. Or at least we didn't. Next thing we know there's an old man, a couple a women and even a little girl standing behind your father, all with guns in hand. That was it for all of us 'cept Clint.

"We backed up our horses and let Clint know we were out. Ridin' for the brand's one thing but women and children? Well, that's something else. But Clint, he was dug in. Couldn't see straight no more and all he knew was killin' your father. He went for his weapon. Now Clint was the fastest I'd ever seen, but your father? Well, he pulled so fast I'm not sure I would have believed it, 'cept that Peacemaker fired a single shot and Clint fell dead.

"By God, Clint's gun hadn't even left his holster. Never seen anything like it. None of us had. Don't know about any of the others, but my hand moved away from my belt. Didn't want there to be any thinkin' I had an interest in pullin'."

Leo nodded his agreement and Timothy added, "Me too. Been riding for a long time. Seen plenty a men good with a gun, but never seen nobody pull like that."

Huck and the other Circle CM men remained silent, taking in this huge piece of news. Huck felt tremendous relief, but it was mixed with an anger at not having been there when his family needed him. He was unable to shake the image of his little sister taking up a gun, though he knew she was capable of it since she wasn't scared of anything or anyone. Just like her mother.

Huck broke the silence. "So what happened next and what's the Circle Y?"

Hank answered. "Otis Randolph, he was Clint's top man, he rode forward toward your father, though I can tell you his hand was nowhere near his gun. Now your father had said to the nine of us that if we swore this was over and that we'd never attack the Circle CM again, he'd let it go.

"Otis said that startin' fresh sounded good to him. We all quickly and happily agreed."

Huck responded, "That sounds like good news, but what's the Boxed Y and what happened to the Boxed X?"

"Turns out Clint had no family and no will. Didn't leave the ranch to anyone. Guess a man like that figures he's never gonna die and even if he does, he doesn't care 'bout anyone after. Circuit judge was riding through town a couple a weeks later and he said maybe the fairest thing was for those of us who'd ridden for the brand to take over the ranch.

"Otis, he's in charge now, but the ranch is all of ours. Never thought I'd own anything more than my gun, my saddle and my horse, so this is an odd thing for all of us. You'll learn when you get home that our ranches work together now. A few of the men still wanted to fight, but we run 'em off and they ain't been seen since. We're down here to pick up some supplies, more than we could get in Bozeman."

Huck looked at each of the three men, still reeling from the news. "You all swear it's the truth?"

Each man nodded.

"You know if I find—"

Timothy spoke. "Huck—all of you—I can see why you might doubt us, but every word is true, 'specially about how fast your father is."

Tom, who hadn't said a word, stood up, reached out his hand to Timothy and said, "Gentlemen, sounds like a tall tale to me, but I can't see how you'd make it up. Only way you'd know how fast Brock could shoot or how easily he could stare down nine of ya is if it happened. Same thing with little Annabelle grabbing a rifle and taking a stand. I think it's best we start fresh. Sure beats the hell outta another gunfight."

Timothy took Tom's hand and when it was over, the men had shaken hands all the way around. After they'd sat back down, Harry asked, "How's it feel? Cowhands all your lives and now owning a piece of—from what I understand —a very large ranch."

Leo, who'd stayed quiet the whole time was the one who answered. "It is a big ranch, but not as big as it was. Turns out Beck was in serious money trouble and died owing quite a few people quite a bit of money. Otis is runnin' the ranch, and he should, but they put me in charge of the money. Always been good with figures. Wasn't sure how we could pay our debts and still operate the ranch.

"Huck, your father came to us, offered a fair price per acre and said he'd buy as many as it took to get us outta debt. We added it up and your father was as good as his word. Now, we're a bit smaller, but none of us owes another man a dollar. And your ranch, the CM, well, it got a bit bigger."

This time it was Jimmy who spoke. "It used to be the Boxed X and now it's the Boxed Y? Why?"

Leo spoke again. "That was Timothy. Said the Boxed X and was done and he wanted to see what came next and since Y comes after..."

The seven men laughed and new friendships were born.

# 20

# PLANS

HUCK KNEW this was excellent news and after what happened in Cheyenne and now with the loss of Enyeto and the injury to Cisco, he knew he needed some good news and assumed everyone else did as well.

It seemed to Huck that it was only a matter of time before there would've been an all-out range war with the Boxed X. To have it end with only the death of Clint Beck, a man Huck thought the world was better off without, was going to make building the ranch and the town that much easier.

He excused himself from the table and went upstairs to check on Cisco and the others. While Sarah and Maddie didn't fully understand the implications of Clint's death, Cisco and Maria did and were relieved.

Cisco remarked, "It will be good to only worry about the weather and the giant bears."

Sarah asked, "How bad of a man was he, this Mr. Beck?"

Huck and Cisco exchanged a glance before Huck began.

"I didn't know the man personally, though I have met others like him. He was big and strong and smart. These are not bad traits in a man, but at some point, he became greedy and the violent. Maybe he always was. Think of a man like Denny Kramer, only with brains, money and power.

"There is a woman you'll meet when we arrive home. Her name is Katie Warner. She is beautiful and smart. She also owns the second biggest ranch in Montana Territory, the Square M. Not only did Katie infuriate Beck by refusing his frequent marriage proposals—some might call them demands—but in his mind she insulted him when her ranch grew to be larger than his. I heard her tell my mother that she thought Beck was going mad. Maybe he was.

"Anyway, Beck's gone now and that's a good thing. A good thing for all of us. The men I just met, they seem like good men, anxious to put the X behind them and live their new lives, riding for the Boxed Y. I have no doubt they are doing so with my mother and father's blessing.

"Also, one other thing. Katie has a sister, Claire. That is the one Tom is sweet on. He'll deny it, but it's true and he can't hide it. She's a wildcat though and while I think she also has an eye for Tom, he's going to have to work to earn her hand."

Maria laughed, which was great for everyone to hear, and added, "She is a beauty. She reminds me of my sister, Cat. A tough woman to catch, but worth it if you can."

Tom, who had come upstairs and caught the tail end of the conversation while standing just outside the door, stepped into the room. "With everything that is happening, this is what you choose to talk about?"

Maddie looked at Tom and then Huck, saying as she did, "Ohh, Huck, you are so right."

Tom's face reddened and he was relieved when Harry and Jimmy followed him into the room a minute later. The two looked around and Jimmy said, "Looks like we walked in on something. Good to see some smiles. As long as we have another day or so before we leave, I was thinking we should probably do some shopping. We'll need to outfit the wagon for Cisco so he can lie down.

"Probably best Maria rides with him. Now that Maddie and Sarah have become pretty good with the wagon, we'll let them handle that. The four of us"—he looked at Harry, Huck and Tom—"will ride horses and keep a lookout. Huck says we're entering Sioux territory, so it's best we be prepared. Clean rifles, plenty of ammunition and enough food and water in case we need to hunker down for a few days."

Huck nodded and began to add to the planning. "Tom,

why don't you head down to the livery. Make sure the wagon's gonna be ready and buy two extra horses. I don't wanna have..."

He stopped, not having meant to upset Maria, but she knew what he meant and told him to continue, taking Cisco's hand as she did.

"I'm sorry Maria, I didn't..."

"It is okay, Huck. It is also true and good planning."

"Okay, thanks. While Tom's doing that, Sarah, you Jimmy and Harry please head down to the general store and pick up some supplies. Plenty to get us home and any extras you see that we'll need once we're there. Make sure everything you buy can fit in the wagon. Need plenty of room for Cisco and Maria. Remember when you're buying that we've got almost three weeks coming up on the trail and though we'll roll through Bozeman before getting home, we need to be prepared."

"Maddie, maybe you can talk to Cisco and Maria and then find the doc and talk to him. Find out everything we're gonna need for Cisco for the trip home and after we get there. Then meet the others at the general store and we'll get everything ready for when we leave."

Sarah looked at Huck and asked, "What are you going to be doing?"

Huck looked at his fiancée and said, "I have a stop to make."

The others could tell that Huck didn't want to share

what he was planning to do and it bothered Sarah, but she respected his obvious need for privacy and knew he would explain when he was ready. No one else said anything.

They walked downstairs together and when they reached the front door, everyone but Huck turned to the right, leading them to the livery and the general store. Huck turned left. He walked to the far end of town and looking up at a simple sign, found what he was looking for. The sign had a single word, not even a name.

'Undertaker.'

# 21

## KENTAKI

Once Huck finished what needed to be done, he turned and walked back toward the hotel. He didn't see any of the others as he came inside, so he decided to sit in the restaurant, enjoy a quiet moment and have a cup of coffee while he waited.

It was only then he remembered the letter he'd been handed in the general store. Meeting the men from the Boxed Y had been his focus in that moment and he'd forgotten about the letter. He reached into his back pocket and was surprised to find it was addressed to him. He was even more surprised to see it had been sent from Hardyville.

That was a place Huck hadn't thought of in a while. He remembered that it was located along the Colorado River in Arizona Territory. A small town that mostly served gold and silver miners who were just starting out, heading into the desert full of dreams and hopes, or those returning, their dreams and hopes having been crushed by the realities of brutal summers, brutal winters, outlaws, Indians and disease.

It was also where he and Brock had met Dario, the man who ran Dario's Mercantile and who gave that up to follow them to Montana. It was also where he and Brock had brought three murderous outlaws to justice for massacring four helpless Hopi Indians, including a woman and her infant son. One of the three they'd had to kill on the way from Hardyville to Fort Mojave, an army outpost also along the Colorado.

The other two came to trial at Fort Mojave. It was where Huck and Brock met then Major Calderwood of the United States Army and then Circuit Court Judge A.F. Ball. Both these men, now known simply as Kevin Calderwood and Alex Ball were waiting in Montana, having become what Huck had come to believe would be an always growing extended family.

Huck opened the letter slowly but found the single page to have survived the trip from Hardyville to Casper. It was dated a month previous.

*Huck, my name is Randolph Vance, though everyone calls me Randy. We do not know each other, but I understand you are traveling with the man who ran this store before me, Dario.*

*Standing in front of me is an Indian from the Havasupai*

*tribe in the Grand Canyon. He says the two of you are friends and he has asked me to write this letter. While his English is surprisingly good, he cannot read or write, at least not English.*

*He said the trip home took almost a month but he was safe and did not go hungry. I'm not sure I understood, but if I did, he traveled almost seven hundred miles by himself from Colorado Territory. You have an impressive friend.*

*It sounds as if all is well with his people. Your other friend, Tochopa?, also made it back safely and is doing well too. I believe his father is the chief, a man named Manakaja? They all miss you and what sounds like a very large family. They especially miss a woman named Pukeheh. I guess she married your grandfather? I'm not sure I'm getting all of this right, but I'm trying and I think I'm close.*

*He wants me to tell you that the canyon is much smaller than he remembers, though it is still beautiful and still home to his people. The chief is staying, along with most of the tribe, but he knows that their days are few. He said to tell you that Tochopa knows all of this but is still staying with his father and their people.*

*He said to tell you that he is going to leave the canyon and travel back to your ranch. He hopes he will be welcome, but his time here has passed. He said it is close to a thousand miles and will take at least two months. He also will not be leaving for a month or two because he wants to help with the spring hunt and leave plenty of meat and jerky for his people.*

*He has told me stories about you and your family, the places you have been, the things you have seen, the battles you have fought. He told me about a grizzly bear. I've never seen one, but when he was done, I have no desire to ever see one.*

*He has left now. He came for supplies for his people. They come about every three months, them and the Hopi. They bring furs and baskets to trade and are always friendly. I hope this letter finds you and I hope your friend makes it all the way to your ranch. The way he described it, it sounds a little bit like heaven. I like the river here, but the desert, I don't know how long I can stay.*

*Oh, and he said to tell your folks and someone named Tom that he said hello.*

*Randy Vance*

*Dario's Mercantile*

*Hardyville*

Huck could hardly have been happier than to think his friend was returning. He'd never let himself hope for that, since Kentaki was so loyal to his people. But, since he had the chief's blessing, he would be returning with a light heart. He wished that Tochopa would too, but he understood how as the chief's son, he felt he had to stay.

Huck also understood what Kentaki meant when he said the canyon seemed small. That was how he felt when he, Kentaki and Tom had visited Dry Springs on their way to Abilene when they picked up Sarah. Even though the town had grown and even prospered, Huck knew right away it was no longer home, at least not for him. That wasn't a bad thing, but he had seen too much since he'd first left. He guessed that was how Kentaki felt, even as beautiful and magnificent as the canyon was.

Huck gently folded the letter and slipped it back in the envelope. He paid for the coffee and was just standing up when his friends walked into the lobby. Huck walked over to meet them and handed Tom the letter as he did.

"Read it when you get a chance. I think you'll like it."

## 22

# OPEN SPACES

As PLANNED, they had ridden and rolled out of Casper two days later. It had taken some creativity to pack everything into the wagon and still leave enough room for Cisco and Maria but they had gotten it done.

They'd been on the trail for three days and had been blessed with excellent weather. It was sunny, but cool. No rain or snow. The terrain was flat, which meant they had good views of everything around them. It was both beautiful and made things a bit safer.

For the first day or two, Huck and the others had felt relatively safe, mostly because they were still so close to Casper. But as each mile passed, he knew they were more likely to run into danger in the form of outlaws or Indians. The Sioux had been making their way west back into the territory and much blood had been spilled. Huck felt it was his job to see that none of that blood came from anyone in his party.

At the same time, he'd taken advantage of the time to teach Sarah how to ride. She and Maddie had become very good with the wagon and took turns with the reins. But Sarah wanted to learn how to ride, really ride. She'd done a little in Abilene, but it was all gentle riding close to or in town. Harry was happy to spend some time in the wagon with Maddie, so he traded places with his daughter, sometimes for hours.

Huck was impressed, and admitting this only to himself, a little surprised, at how quickly and easily Sarah learned. By the end of the second day, she was galloping at full speed, laughing loudly as she did. Huck made sure they stayed close to the wagon since his primary responsibility was the safety of the group, but a couple of times, they rode a mile or two away.

As the sun set on the third day, Sarah turned to Huck and said, "Huck, I love this life. Will it always be like this?"

Huck smiled at his fiancée and answered, "In part, yes, it will always be like this. Living outside of a town is different than living in one. Where we're going is just as open as this and maybe even prettier. There is more land and fewer people than you are used to. That can be good and bad.

"We have freedoms that those who live in towns don't have. There is a beauty to the solitude and the quiet. But,

Sarah, it also means we have only ourselves to rely on. There are no doctors when we get sick. No sheriffs or marshals to turn to if there is trouble. No restaurants or general stores or shops, at least not without a few days' ride.

"There are outlaws and Indians. You heard what happened with my father and the man who owned the Boxed X. That was something we had to take care of ourselves. The Sioux are making trouble, more every day, and we're going to have to deal with that. The weather is worse than you're used to, especially in the winter.

"But, Sarah, it is worth it. Worth the risk and the danger. I don't think I could ever live in a big city. I haven't yet, but I have visited more than a couple of larger towns and I felt suffocated. I don't think I could even live in a town again. I loved living in Dry Springs, but there is something about knowing everything that needs to be done, you need to do. That every day is a struggle, a danger and a joy...

"I don't know how to explain it. I can only hope you love it as much as I do."

She took his hand and looked into his eyes, saying, "I think you have explained it perfectly, and I am sure that I will love it as much as you do, as much as I love you."

Before Huck could say anything, Maddie spoke. "Forgive me, but I couldn't help but overhear. Where we are going, is it really as remote as you say?"

This got everyone's attention and Huck looked around before answering.

"It is. You're originally from Pittsburgh, right?"

"Yes, I am."

"I've never been back east. Never seen what you would call a city. Biggest place I've ever seen was Los Angeles in California. Didn't live there, just traveled through, but they say there are five thousand people living there. How many people live in Pittsburgh?"

"My father said we had more than eighty thousand people."

Huck whistled and added, "I haven't seen eighty thousand people in my entire life. I haven't seen maybe ten thousand people." Huck turned to Harry. "How many people would you say live in Abilene?"

"In town? We have two thousand or more, maybe gettin' close to three thousand if you count the surrounding ranches and farms. Also have about five thousand cowboys come through each of the last couple a years."

Huck nodded and continued, "Maddie, where we're going, there are about thirty people, countin' everyone here. We have some ranches close and by close I mean a half day to a couple a days' ride. And we're building a town just a handful a miles away from the main ranch. But I wouldn't think that town would have a hundred people living in it for at least for a couple a years.

"Biggest town close to us is Bozeman. It's a three- or

four-day ride, and I'm guessin' there's less than two hundred people livin' there. Bunch more on the ranches around there, places like ours, but nothing like what you've seen."

Maddie looked around and no one could tell if she was happy or concerned. "Thirty people? Counting us?"

Huck answered, "Yep."

"I had more than thirty students in my school back in Pennsylvania."

It was Harry who spoke next. "Jimmy, you didn't tell your fiancée what she was gettin' herself in for before you packed her up and headed north?"

Before Jimmy could answer, Maddie did while laughing. "No, Harry, he told me. I'm not sure I understood, but he told me. The thing is, until today, until tonight, until right now, I really didn't know what that meant. I've never seen anything like this. We've been riding for three days and we haven't seen another person. Not one."

Jimmy started to look concerned, then turned and faced his fiancée. "Maddie..."

She smiled, took his hand and said, "Jimmy, I've never seen anything more beautiful, been more excited or felt more alive than I do right now. Thank you for bringing me."

Jimmy wanted to be happy, but for the moment, he was just tremendously relieved.

# 23

# BURIAL

THE FOLLOWING MORNING, they'd been moving for less than an hour when suddenly Maddie and Sarah heard a gasp from Maria. Fearing something had happened with Cisco, they stopped the wagon and within seconds all four men had ridden close, rifles ready.

Sarah looked at Cisco and didn't see anything different than she'd seen for the past few days, but still she asked, "Cisco, are you okay?"

"Yes, I am fine. It's my... What's wrong, Maria?"

By now, Maria was crying, close to sobbing, though she was obviously trying not to. The way she sat in the wagon, her back leaning against the front boards, she could only see what was behind them, what they had already rolled past. Unable to speak, she simply pointed back and to the left. With tremendous effort, enough to cause him quite a bit of pain, Cisco sat upright. He looked back and instantly, it was obvious he was hurting too.

"It is our Enyeto." He pointed in the same direction as Maria. "He is buried there."

Sarah and Maddie locked the wagon in place and quickly climbed into the back, squeezing out enough room so they could both hold and comfort Maria. Huck turned Spirit and took off toward the spot, followed by Tom. Jimmy and Harry stayed close to the wagon.

The little burial spot was under one of the only trees in the area. He was not buried deeply and the grave was covered with a few rocks. There were signs that scavengers had tried to get to Enyeto, but the rocks Maria had stacked had done their job.

Huck turned to Tom, saying, "We have two shovels in the wagon. Please go get them and ask the others to wait."

Without a word, Tom did as he was asked and was back in only a couple of minutes. Knowing what Huck had in mind, he slipped off his horse, handing one of the shovels to Huck who was already on the ground. They started work, digging a proper grave. The ground was not soft and it took almost an hour.

As hard as that was, it was not nearly as hard as having to dig up Enyeto's broken body and place it in the new grave. They carefully covered him and then, as Maria had done, covered the grave with rocks. When they were finally done, Huck rode back and asked everyone to join them. The ground was flat enough that the wagon had no trouble and soon everyone except Cisco was standing around the freshly dug grave.

Cisco insisted that Huck and Tom help him down from the wagon. Maria, Sarah and Maddie argued that he shouldn't, that the doctor said he shouldn't stand for weeks, but he insisted. "A man should never have to see his child buried. But if he does, he needs to stand and show the child, and God, the respect."

The women had nothing more to say. It wound up taking all four men to get Cisco to the ground. Using the wagon to keep himself upright and with tears rolling down his face, he started to speak.

"My dear Enyeto. I am so sorry that this happened and that you died. I knew the riding was dangerous, but it made you so happy. I never could say no to you. You were the best little boy any man could ask for.

"I wish you had known your real father, P'oe. He was a great man and my best friend. He had such dreams for you and your mother, and he would have made them come true. He was smart and brave, just like you, Enyeto. He would have loved you so much, just like I did.

"Your mother is here, Enyeto. She is even braver than your father. No mother ever loved a child more than she loved you, little man. We are going to have a baby, Enyeto. You would have had a baby brother, or maybe a baby sister, but you wouldn't have been the baby anymore. I know you would have loved and taught the baby so much. How to play. How to love. How to feed the chickens. How to sneak hard candies when you didn't think we were looking."

The tears overtook Cisco and he stopped, held on one side by Huck and on the other by Tom. They didn't notice at first, but soon everyone realized that Maria was talking. She was talking very quietly in Spanish, which none of them except Cisco understood. Every once in a while, they would hear her say Cisco, P'oe or Enyeto, but the rest was between her, Cisco and Enyeto. As it should be.

When she was done and before they loaded Cisco back into the wagon, Huck asked Harry to take his place holding Cisco upright and signaled for Jimmy to help him with something in the wagon.

It was in the very back, wrapped in blankets and when they went to move it, Jimmy was surprised by how heavy it was. But when the blankets slipped off, he saw and understood. They worked it toward the front of the wagon, then both jumped down and lifted it up, carrying it very gently to where Enyeto lay buried.

The others could now see that it was a headstone. It was arched and cut out of marble. It was why Huck had gone to the undertaker. They placed it on top of the grave, moving the rocks so that it fit and was raised above every-thing else. It said:

*Enyeto Hinojosa*
*1868-1873*
*Loving son of*
*Cisco, Maria & P'oe*

## 24

# DUST

THE REST OF THE DAY, while as beautiful as the previous days had been, didn't feel like that to any of the travelers. The sun's warmth did not seem to reach as deep, food tasted bland, and conversation (when there was any) was short, humorless and functional.

The reason was obvious. Enyeto.

They'd all known he'd been killed. They had grieved for him, as well as Cisco and Maria. But somehow, seeing the tiny little grave, knowing he'd been out there all by himself and now would be forever, hit them much harder than any of them had expected. In a way, Maria seemed more upset now than when they first saw her in Casper.

Huck thought it might have been that because before that, she had been forced to focus on saving Cisco and then on his recovery and wasn't allowed the kind of grieving a mother needs. Either Sarah or Maddie was in the wagon with her most of the time, since even the effort to get out of the wagon for a few minutes set Cisco back and he had been sleeping since they left the gravesite.

Huck signaled for Tom, Harry and Jimmy to join him at the point. When the four were gathered, he looked back at the wagon, with Maddie on the reins and the other three in the back.

"I know this is hard on everyone. But the farther we are from Casper, the more danger we are in. While I understand what they are going through... Well, maybe I don't, but I'm trying. Doesn't matter, though. We can let those on the wagon be, but we have to pay even more attention to the things around us.

"Tom and I have been attacked by both outlaws and Indians on this very trail, and it would take incredibly good fortune for that not to happen again. Harry, Jimmy, you're both good men and I'd feel good having you stand with me in about any situation. But trail life is different than town life and trail problems are different than town problems."

Harry asked, "Huck, what are you asking from us? What's different?"

"Outlaws, they're actually more obvious here than in town. In town, you knew most everyone and you learned to trust them and to trust their friends. You know the ones who live in town that you need to be careful of and you can pay attention to anyone who's new.

"Out here, it's best you assume the worst in people. Hate to say that, but it's true. We've met good people on the trail but Brock taught me to keep my eyes open and my hand near my gun until I know for sure. You see a group of men ridin' together, no women, no children? Expect them to cause some trouble until they're long gone, or you get to know 'em well enough to trust 'em. Even then, be careful.

"Other thing is, in town, you can count on some help from the people who live there. Out here, it's just us. Just the four of us. And we can't all be together all the time."

Jimmy nodded his understanding and asked, "And Indians?"

"Worse. They're quieter and sneakier than anyone you've ever met in town. At least the bad ones are. There are good Indians—and I've met plenty—but I've also met enough of the others that I sleep every night on the trail with one eye open, sometimes two. They can hide in places you'd never think they could. They can ride better than any of us. They don't usually have good weapons, but they're good with what they have.

"They don't have any rules. Kill you any way they can. Kill women and children as easy as you'd kill a sick dog. Jimmy, you're gonna have to have a tough talk with Maddie. Make sure she has a gun with her at all times. If things go terrible and we're gonna be run over, she's gonna have to use it rather than be taken. You understand?"

Jimmy just sat there for a moment. His jaw dropped

and the others could see him thinking about what Huck had said. "I do. I mean, I guess I do. Never thought about that before. Sarah? Maria?"

Huck answered, "Maria knows; she's been out here before. Sarah? I'm gonna talk to her when we stop. Thing is, startin' now, we gotta be looking at all times. We'll ride closer to the wagon, one on each side, one out front and one tailing. You see anything different, anything that catches your attention, ride back toward the wagon, but slowly. Won't do to let them know you've seen something.

"Now, I'll take the point. Most likely they'll be waiting for us. Tom'll drag behind in case they try and come up behind us. Less likely comin' at us from the sides but that don't mean they won't. We've got about three hours 'til the sun sets.

"First good spot I find, we'll stop and set up for the night. Best to eat and have camp ready before dark. Startin' tonight, we'll each be on watch. Two at a time, half night sleep for each of us. We'll be tired, but havin' two guards is important. If you don't have any questions, let's get going. Stay close enough you can see two of us at all times and never let the wagon out of your sight."

Ninety minutes later, Huck pulled up and waited for the wagon and the other three riders to join. When they did, he said, "This'll do for tonight. Small hill here we can tuck the wagon next to and one of the guards can stay on top. Give us a good view all around. Sarah, Maddie, startin' now you'll be in charge of meals. Tom, Jimmy, you stay here. Look after your horses and keep your eyes open. Harry, you come with me. We'll ride for a bit and have a look around. Jimmy, you need to talk to Maddie."

Everyone understood and got to work. Harry and Tom started to ride and they hadn't gone far at all when Harry said, "Huck, my old eyes may be getting bad, but if you look east a little bit, you see some dust rising? Could be a small desert wind, but..."

Huck pulled up and stared in the direction Harry pointed.

"Not like any wind I've ever seen. Best we head back."

# 25

## VISITORS

HARRY AND HUCK pulled back into the makeshift camp, surprising everyone and concerning some.

Huck pulled everyone together around the wagon. "I was hoping this wasn't going to happen at all and certainly not this soon, but we've got visitors on the way."

Sarah and Maddie gasped, but Maria had been through too much in the past few years and would wait before growing too concerned.

When Huck pointed east, they could all see the dust and could tell it was coming directly for them. Huck continued, "Just from what we've seen, we know a few things. First, and this is good news, it's not Indians. No way they'd be riding straight at us and no way they'd be giving us such an obvious sign.

"We don't know how many and we don't know what they want, if anything. Might just be traveling through, no different than us. Might be trouble. Until we know, we'll assume it's trouble. Jimmy, you take a rifle and climb on top of that small hill. Don't come down unless we call you and stay out of sight. Whoever's coming might not be the only ones, so you'll need to keep a lookout for others, as well as watching what's happening here. You'll be the only one on lookout, so be careful.

"Harry, I want you up in the wagon with Cisco and Maria. Sarah and Maddie, quickly heat up some beans and steak, but when these folks get here, make your way back to the wagon. Tom, you'll stay between the wagon and whoever rides in. You can sit and eat, but don't let them get between you and the wagon. I'll stay right here by the fire. If they don't start any trouble, I'll offer them something to eat, but I'll make sure that after that, they're on their way. No one's staying here with us. Questions?"

Cisco's head slowly lifted over the top of the wagon. By his face, they could all tell how much it hurt to do so. He looked at Huck. "Where's my gun?"

Huck started to answer, but Maria, with pride in her voice said, "I'll get my husband his gun."

Jimmy started for the top of the little hill, Sarah and Maddie started cooking and Harry, Huck and Tom checked their weapons.

TWENTY MINUTES LATER, two men rode close enough to be seen. Huck and Tom set down their plates and adjusted their gun belts as one of the men called out, "Hello, the camp! Like to ride in."

Huck called back, "You're welcome to but walk in those horses and keep your hands where we can see them."

The same man yelled again, "Not sounding too friendly."

Huck immediately answered, "Don't know you and wasn't expecting anyone. If you don't like my manners, you're welcome to keep riding. If you're friendly and hungry, you can join us, but like I said, walking in and with hands empty except for your horses' reins. Up to you."

"We're coming in."

The two men walked in, each with one hand on a rein and the other one clear and empty. Huck looked at them and said, "You can tie 'em off on the wagon or stake 'em if you prefer. Got plenty a beans and antelope steak if you're interested."

The second of the two men answered, "Thank ya, mister. We're plenty hungry. I think we'll stake the horses, let 'em eat same time we do." Once they'd staked the horses, they walked into camp, hands empty. The second one said, "My name's Bart and this is Owen."

Huck introduced everyone, except Jimmy who was

lying down on top of the hill, hopefully out of sight as Huck had warned him. He handed both man a plate and a fork and pointed to the food staying warm over the fire. They each dished up a plate and took a seat.

Tom joined them around the fire as Huck asked, "Where you boys headed?"

Bart answered, "South. Casper. After that, Texas."

"Where you coming from?"

"Up north. Did some trapping around the Fort Peck Reservation, close to Canada."

"Good trapping?"

"There was, but time to head back to Texas. Too cold for us up here. How 'bout you? Which way you going?"

"Heading north. Heard it's pretty up there. Guess Bozeman's our next stop."

The four men finished their meals in silence. Huck noticed that the two took in everything about the camp and more than once caught them staring at the wagon. It could have been the supplies or the women, or maybe both, that caught their interest, but Huck didn't like the way they looked. He certainly didn't get a good feeling about either man, though neither had said anything aggressive or offensive. Still, it didn't hurt to be cautious.

As they finished up their dinner, Huck stood up, and Tom did the same.

Bart said, "Thanks for the chow. Tasted plenty good."

"You're welcome. Looks like your horses got their fill

too. About time for you boys to be riding on now. Hope the rest of your trip is safe."

Owen looked around and said, "Thought maybe we'd sleep here tonight. Heard there's Injuns around and maybe we'd all be safer that way."

Huck shook his head and answered, "Thanks, but we'll take our chances. Again, you have a safe ride."

Huck watched as the smiles left Bart's and Owen's faces, if only for a moment. What he saw was ugly. Owen looked directly at Huck. "Doesn't seem too friendly."

"We fed ya and that seems plenty friendly to me. It's a big territory. You won't have trouble finding a place to sleep."

As Bart and Owen turned toward their horses, Owen looked back over his shoulder and without even a hint of a smile, said, "Maybe we'll see you again." They gathered up their horses and rode out, back east the way they came.

When they were out of earshot, Huck waved Jimmy down. When everyone was gathered again around the wagon, Huck spoke.

"We'll see those men again. There'll be others with them and they won't be as friendly."

Sarah asked, "How do you know?"

"They said they were coming from the north but rode in from the east. They didn't have bedrolls, any packed food and certainly no signs of being trappers. That means it's all waiting for them somewhere and there's no reason to have left it, 'less someone was watchin' it. When they left, they headed back the way they came, not south like they said. No, there's others out there and these two were scoutin' us.

"Don't know if it'll be tonight, or if they'll wait 'til morning, but they'll be back."

# 26

# READY

HUCK WATCHED until the men were out of sight. When they were, he turned back to the group, saying, "It's too late for us to leave tonight. We wouldn't be able to outrun them anyway. I'm tempted for a couple of us to follow them and maybe take care of it before they can come back. But we don't know how many there are, and I hate to split us up.

"So, we're gonna keep this simple. We'll clear some stuff out of the back of the wagon. Make enough room for Sarah and Maddie to sleep up there with Cisco and Maria. Rifles for everyone. Harry, you and Tom'll spend the night on top of the hill. If one of you gets tired, go ahead and catch a little nap, but the other needs to keep watching. If they do come back, no guarantee it'll be from the same direction, or that they won't split up and come back from more than one direction.

"Jimmy, you and I will wait and watch right here. The wagon should be pretty safe and we'll stay between it and the plains. I figure there's four, maybe five of them. When they come back, they won't be asking nicely to come into camp."

Everyone was looking at each other and then back to Huck.

Maddie asked, "Are you sure they're coming back?"

"I'm not. But if I was sitting at a table, I'd bet a lot that they would be. Nothing about them seemed right and we have plenty a things here to attract their attention."

Jimmy asked, "How do we know when to fire?"

Huck looked at Jimmy and then Tom. "Tom, you remember those rustlers when we were pushing the cattle?"

"Of course."

"Remember how Gus taught us you can't give men like that a chance? That they'd been warned and how as soon as we saw them, we started firing?"

"I do."

"Well, it's the same thing here. Harry, Jimmy, this is different than in town. No one's gonna help us and there's no need and no time to issue a warning. If those men come back, it'll be with evil intent. I aim to end it before they get a chance to hurt any of us. I'm hoping we won't have to fire at all, but if we do, best if I be the first. But once I start, or any of us does, we all keep shooting until it's over. And out here, now, over means they're all dead."

Huck waited as he looked at every member of the group. When no one said anything, he asked, "Does everyone understand? Anyone have a problem or want to discuss this?"

Maddie, leaning over the side of the wagon, seemed shocked and asked, "Are you really gonna kill those men if they come back?"

This time it was Tom who answered. "Miss Maddie, we are. We have to. If we don't, they'll kill us, or worse. You may not have understood it, but Huck warned 'em when they were leaving and they heard it too. Huck's right. They do come back? It's to do us harm. Best thing we can do is stop that before they can. I know how you're feeling. I went it through it myself not too long ago. But like Huck said, this isn't Abilene or Pittsburgh. This is the prairie. We're alone, except for each other and we need to take care of ourselves. It's hard, but it's the life we've chosen."

Jimmy looked around. "Huck, we should have some time before they come back, if they do. Right?"

"We do. They rode in from pretty far off. They'll need to ride back, make plans and then return. They may even wait 'til morning."

"Okay then. Maddie, if you'd come down from there, maybe we can take a short walk?" He turned toward Huck.

"We'll stay close. I'll have my rifle and we won't go out of sight."

Huck nodded.

WHILE JIMMY and Maddie took a walk, Huck helped Sarah down from the wagon and they sat around the fire. Huck took Sarah's hand.

"Sarah, I know this is a lot to take in. It's different than anything you've ever known. Up until three or four years ago, I couldn't imagine it myself. But there really is no other way. I've been thinking though, maybe this isn't what you signed up for. When this is over, if you want, I'll bring you back to Abilene. I'll understand. I really will. It's not for everyone."

Sarah took her other hand and with both, wrapped up Huck's non-gun hand.

"When you wrote me that letter, the one that talked about you killing those rustlers, without so much as a warning..."

Huck started to interrupt, but Sarah stopped him and kept going.

"I know, Gus told 'em if they followed you, you'd kill 'em on sight. That they'd had their warning and there wouldn't be another one. I cried for three nights. I didn't understand. I'd never heard anything like that. It didn't make me question my love for you, but it made me wonder if I was cut out for this life. If I could do what you did or live with you if you had to do it over again.

"On the fourth day, I went to my father and showed him the letter. I told him my thoughts and asked him for his. In my whole life, he's never let me down. It's been me and him since my mom died and the truth is, Huck, if he'd said I couldn'ta married you, I don't think I would have.

"But he did give his approval. And when he read your letter, I think it made him feel even stronger about you. He told me that you were right, that things are different out here and that I needed to be okay with that. That there wasn't always a way, or the time, to have a trial with a jury and a judge.

"He also told me how much he respected how you struggled with what you did. You and Tom. He said he knew then, beyond any doubt, what kind of man you were and how far you would go to protect me, which he said is a man's job.

"I'm telling you this because I hate what we're going to have to do, but I understand, and if it comes to it, I'll be right by your side. I'll reload your guns, I'll patch anyone up who gets hurt, and they get close enough"—here she pulled out an 1849 Colt pocket pistol—"I'll shoot 'em myself. Harry was teaching me while you were gone."

Huck shook his head in surprise and said, "That was my first gun. Where...?"

"My father. He said I should have it. I should have told you sooner, but I just didn't think about it until tonight. I know my father is having this same talk with Maddie right now and maybe she'll stay and maybe she'll need to go back. If not all the way to Pittsburgh, at least back to Abilene. But me? I'm with the man I'm going to spend the rest of my life with. It's the life I've chosen and one we'll build together."

Huck wrapped his arms around Sarah and wondered how he had gotten so lucky.

# 27

## MORNING

JIMMY RETURNED with Maddie and walked her to the wagon at the same time Huck did with Sarah. Huck turned to Jimmy and said, "Let's go ahead and mount up. We'll stay within sight of the wagon, but we'll be able to move quickly if we need to."

This night benefited the hunted. The moon was large and bright and there was no wind, so sound would carry far and easily. It was cool without being cold, which was good because they were not going to have a fire.

Huck explained to Jimmy about trusting your vision and looking for any movement. It was often easier to detect off to the side than looking straight ahead. After a bit of silence, he continued, "I'm guessing your conversation with Miss Maddie was similar to the one I had with Sarah?"

"I'm guessin' so. She's pretty shaken up by all of this. The romance of the wild West is a lot different when looked at from the safety of your Pittsburgh home while having dinner with friends, or even than it was in Abilene. I was thinkin' I hadn't done a good job of explaining to her what she was in for. 'Bout what might happen out here and how it would feel. But then I got to thinkin', maybe I hadn't really it understood myself."

Huck, his eyes never stopping scanning the prairie, answered, "Mine was worse. I knew and I still didn't tell your Sarah enough. I think it was because we just haven't had that much time together, but truth is, maybe I was afraid it would scare her off."

"Did it?"

"It did not. You raised one tough girl, Mr. Huckaby. Forgive me for saying so, but she has sand. Reminds me of my mother and that's just about the highest compliment I know to give a woman. Heck, anyone. How about Miss Maddie?"

"Can't say she isn't scared, though I guess we all are. At least Sarah saw a little of this in Abilene. Cowboys get a little wild and sometimes men get killed. But Maddie, she never saw any of this. But she's tough, maybe tougher than she knows, and she wants to stick it out. Told her I'd bring her back to Abilene, even Pittsburgh if she wanted, and I'd stick with her no matter what, no matter where."

"I told Sarah the same thing."

"And?"

"Heck, she's tougher than I am and she's staying. Miss Maddie?"

"I'm not saying she didn't think about it. Guess anyone would. But she said she came out here for an adventure and this certainly is one. She's staying. So I guess we both did pretty well. Now we gotta protect 'em. Protect 'em with our lives."

"Mr. Huckaby, I hope you know by now that I will do anything for your daughter. If I didn't tell you before, I'm tellin' you now. I appreciate that you gave me a chance. Not everyone would have and you didn't have to. I know I'm young, but I've seen and done more things than most men ever will.

"And one thing I've seen is how Brock treats my mother. How he treats family. She's gonna have everything I can possibly give her and have the best life she can possibly have. That was my promise to her and it's my promise to you."

"I know that, son. That's why I agreed to let her come. 'Course, on the other hand, I ain't so trustin' I'da let her come without me."

Both men laughed, quietly, and Huck suggested they ride back closer to the wagon.

The hours passed without incident, though more than once the men thought they saw something. A man's eyes can play tricks on him and even more so when he's tired and maybe a little bit scared. None of the four men slept a wink and even the girls slept very little.

As the pre-dawn light started to creep in from the east, Huck called Harry and Tom down from the hill and had everyone quickly pack up. They skipped breakfast and were rolling north before dawn.

As they started, Harry asked, "Huck, thought you said we couldn't outrun 'em?"

"We can't. There's no way. But we're not gonna just sit here all day and wait for 'em either. Not sure if it's true, but they said they were headin' south. Maybe they'll ride back to where we were and figure it's not worth chasin' us and just keep riding. They certainly saw we have four well-armed men. Sometimes that'll discourage people. If not, we'll deal with it when we see 'em."

Maddie had the reins and Huck turned toward Sarah and Maria, saying, "Sarah, you keep your eyes looking east. You see anything, anything at all, you call us in. Maria, you keep looking behind us. Most likely place they'll be comin' from. Tom, you ride on our right side; Jimmy, you got the left; and Harry, you're out front. Stay close to the wagon and within shouting distance of each other. Anything happens, gather 'round the wagon and start shooting. Like I said yesterday, don't stop 'til they're all..."

Tom asked, "What about you, Huck?"

"I'm gonna drift back and keep an eye open behind us. Men like that aren't usually big planners, usually just figger they can scare people and if not, they can kill 'em. They might just come ridin' up behind us."

Huck patted his rifle scabbard, which held a brand new Winchester 1873 lever action rifle he'd bought in Abilene. He'd been practicing quite a bit and knew he was both fast and accurate. He had plenty of ammo and thought he might be able to discourage anyone who was following.

Jimmy was surprised by this and said so. "You're headin' back to face these men alone? Doesn't make any sense, Huck."

Before Huck could answer, Tom did. "Mr. Huckaby, Huck's right. We need men close to the wagon. Those men could come from any direction. There could be other men we know nothin' about and there's always the chance of Indians. Wish we had more men and more time, but we don't have neither. I've seen Huck in tough spots before. Except for Brock and maybe Gus, there might not be anyone better. If he can back them down, he will. If he can't, you'll see how fast Spirit can run and we'll be here waiting."

Harry, as much to himself as to the anyone else, said, "This sure as hell ain't like nothin' I've ever seen."

# 28

# BART

It was late morning when they stopped for breakfast. They'd been rolling for close to five hours and Huck was optimistic that he'd either misjudged the men, or they'd been discouraged by the distance and continued south, if that really was the direction they had been travelling.

Since they had no way to hide anyway, Huck agreed to a fire, and Maddie and Sarah worked to put together a nice breakfast. They had the last of the eggs they'd purchased in Casper, plenty of beans, and fresh antelope steaks. Add to that some hot coffee, with some of the honey they'd also picked up in Casper, and it tasted like a feast.

The weather remained in their favor. Sunny, cool and no wind. They seemed to talk about almost anything other than what was obviously on everyone's mind. Maddie was the first to address the obvious. "Huck, do you think maybe we won't see those men again?"

"I wish I could tell you yes, but too many times I've been surprised by men and the things they're willing to do. I will say I feel better with each passing mile and each passing hour, at least with regards to those men. Keep in mind though, it won't do for us to take anything for granted until we're safely back at the ranch. Between here and there, plenty can happen. 'Course, it's possible for nothing to happen and we can keep prayin' for that."

Huck had barely finished when Cisco called out from the wagon. "Huck, best you look behind us."

With a bad feeling, Huck turned around and saw what Cisco was looking at. A steady dust cloud. Still a ways off, but bigger than the one that Owen and Bart had stirred up yesterday. Whoever they were, they were coming from the south, so Huck guessed it was the men he feared would follow. They had probably done exactly what Huck had said they might. Ride in from the east. Find the wagon gone and very easily follow the tracks north. It appeared to Huck they were making no effort to hide their presence.

While Huck and the others stared at the dust, Tom, who had the best eyesight of them all, looked carefully in each of the other three directions, then said, "Huck, I can't see anyone else coming. If they are, they're a ways off or far more careful than those riding behind us. Looks like five to me, but I'll know for sure in a couple a minutes."

"Thanks, Tom. Do me a favor, mount up and keep an eye out for everyone and anyone. The rest of us, let's move stuff around in the wagon and see if we can't make it safer. Stack stuff against the sides. Also, let's turn it around so the front is facing whoever's coming."

It only took a few minutes. Just as they were finishing up, Tom called out, "Still can't see anyone except those coming straight at us and yay, it's five of 'em."

"Okay, everyone needs to have a rifle. Sarah, Maddie, Maria and Cisco, you stay in the wagon. Jimmy, you stay with them. Harry, you mount up. Me, you and Tom'll ride out a bit and see if we can't change their minds."

Jimmy responded immediately. "I'm not staying here while you three ride out to meet 'em. No way in hell."

Huck turned his horse and faced him. "Mr. Huckaby, I'm gonna listen to you about a lot a things, most especially about your daughter. But out here, only one man can be in charge. We agreed back in Abilene that that was gonna be me. I've been through this more than once and my father, Brock, is the best I've ever seen at handling these things. But he'd never, never, ride out and leave the women alone.

"And Mr. Huckaby, if you're wondering why you're the one staying, it's not because I don't think you can handle yourself out here or lack the sand to stand up to these men. It's exactly the opposite. That's your daughter and your fiancée in that wagon.

"No man will be more motivated to defend them than

you. Cisco, no offense made and I know you'd die to protect these women, but you're hurtin'. Hate being so blunt and wish we had more time to talk about this, but we don't.

"Now, we'll be between the wagon and these men. If shootin' starts, they'll probably split up and come at us from multiple directions. As soon as you have a shot, start takin' it, and like I said, don't stop 'til they're all dead. And as for the shootin', you hear one, that means it's started."

As unhappy as he looked, Jimmy nodded, so did Cisco. Huck pointed Spirit toward the incoming men. Tom took up on his left and Harry on his right. All three had cocked rifles laying across their legs, ready in an instant. Huck's 1873 had a full 14-round magazine and both Tom and Harry had Henry rifles. Huck knew from his practice rounds that he was very accurate up to a hundred yards and fairly accurate for another fifty beyond that.

When the men were about two hundred yards apart, Huck, Tom and Harry pulled up. Each of them pointed their rifle forward, leaving no doubt about their intent. The five men took another seventy-five yards before coming to a stop.

Huck could see Bart and Owen and yelled across, "You come all this way to thank us for the meal last night?"

The five men exchanged glances with each other and then Bart, who was in the center, yelled back, "Figured maybe you got enough left for a mid-day meal. Like I said, we're short on grub and that was some good eats last night."

"Afraid we can't help you this time. Didn't plan on so many extra mouths to feed and got just about enough for ourselves and that's it. You can turn right around and ride to Casper. Leave now and you'll get there before you have to tighten up your belts too much."

Bart stood up in his stirrups and then called across, "Thing is, none of us like being hungry, even a little. How 'bout we come in, take what we need in food and supplies and then we ride on?"

Huck didn't move, he simply said, "No."

"No? That ain't too friendly."

"We were friendly last night and I'm not real fond of how you're trying to repay us, so no."

"Maybe we'll have to kill you, at least the men, and then take everything."

So fast that none of the other men had time to move, including Tom and Harry, Huck raised his Winchester and fired a single shot.

# 29

## TOM

BART SLIPPED SLOWLY from his horse, a bullet wound in the center of his chest and his filthy brown shirt slowly being covered by the spreading blood. The seven living men stared as Bart fell with a look of surprise on his face. He crashed onto the prairie floor, a small cloud of dust rising as he did. The men had all seen enough death to know that Bart wasn't getting up—ever.

The outlaws, overly confident, hadn't even pulled their rifles from their scabbards. Maybe they thought the banter between Bart and Huck would continue for a while longer, or maybe they thought the men really would back down and simply give them what they wanted. But the banter ended for Huck the moment Bart threatened the women. The men with him never had any intention of backing down.

The outlaws had been in tough spots before. They were hardened men and this wasn't the first time they'd been shot at or had shot to kill. They pulled their pistols in a flash and fired as though their lives depended on it. Which they did.

Maybe it was because he was a familiar face, or they felt a sense of direct betrayal since the night before they had fed him, but both Tom and Harry fired at Owen. One or both of the men hit him, and he joined Bart on the ground.

Huck charged the three remaining outlaws. One of the three broke toward the right and tried to circle around toward the wagon. Huck trusted that Jimmy and the others would take care of him. Shots were ringing out, but shooting straight from a galloping horse is tough, and for a moment the remaining men were still in their saddles. Harry and Tom quickly joined Huck in charging forward while the outlaws stayed put.

Huck watched in horror as Tom toppled from his horse and followed Bart and Owen onto the prairie dirt.

Jimmy tore his eyes from what was happening in front of him and yelled at the others in the wagon to do the same. They listened and turned to face the oncoming outlaw. What the man expected to find will never be known but there was no way he knew he would be riding into the furious fire of five rifles. He didn't have a chance and fell under the barrage of bullets. Sadly his horse joined him in death, though that was certainly accidental.

When the man was down, Jimmy took his time sighting in and fired two more bullets into him, remembering what Huck had said about making sure they were all dead. When he finished, he turned back to Huck, Harry and Tom. He saw Tom on the ground and watched as Harry and Huck quickly finished off the two remaining outlaws.

Jimmy and Sarah leapt from the wagon at the same time and raced across the prairie until they reached Tom. Maddie made sure Cisco and Maria were okay, relieved that neither had been hit. Huck and Harry checked to be sure the four outlaws were dead, which they were, and Huck yelled to Harry, "Make sure the last one is dead."

Harry took off without a word and Huck jumped from Spirit and raced to Tom. He saw the same thing Jimmy and Sarah had already seen. Tom was bleeding. They could see he'd been shot in the shoulder, but didn't know if he'd been hit anywhere else, or if he was even alive. Huck, who had lost too many friends over the years, had to stop himself from throwing up at the sight of his childhood friend lying motionless, his eyes closed, blood flowing.

"Tom! Dammit, Tom, are you okay?"

Tom's eyes slowly opened and the slightest of smiles came to his face. "I might be, if you'd stop shaking me."

Huck hadn't realized he'd been shaking his friend, which couldn't have made the shoulder feel any better. He smiled back, relieved his friend was alive.

"Wouldn'ta had to shake you if you weren't lying here

napping while we were in the middle of a gunfight. We can see the shoulder. Anywhere else?"

"Not that I can tell. The shoulder hurts plenty enough, though."

"Jimmy, help me roll him over and let's see if that bullet went straight through. Sarah, you go back to the wagon, get some water boilin' and have the others start making room for Tom in the back with Cisco."

As gently as they could, Jimmy and Huck rolled Tom over. Huck was relieved to see that the bullet had gone clean through. A quick look didn't show any other wounds and Huck knew his friend could survive a shot to the shoulder.

"Tom, me and Jimmy are gonna try to get you standing and move you back to the wagon. They're getting some water boiling so we can clean you up and they're making some room in the wagon so you can lie around and do nothin' for the next couple a days."

"And have to listen to you for the next couple a years talking 'bout how I didn't carry my load? No way. It's my left shoulder. Let's get it patched up. I'll still be able to ride and shoot."

Jimmy looked at Tom and then Huck, and then laughed. "He's gonna be just fine. Now, let's get him to the wagon."

Jimmy and Huck half carried Tom as he tried to walk. It wasn't far and soon he was slumped against the side of the wagon. Maddie and Sarah stripped off his jacket and shirt and started cleaning the wound. Maddie had never seen a gunshot wound before and everyone was impressed at how well she was handling everything.

As they finished up, with Huck hovering over them the entire time, Sarah stood up. As she did, Huck started to fall and Sarah screamed.

# 30

# HUCK

JIMMY AND HARRY managed to catch Huck before he fell. As they helped him to the ground, they could both see why Sarah had screamed.

Huck's leg was covered in blood.

Maria climbed down from the wagon, where her injured husband lay, to help Maddie clean and bandage Tom's wound. As soon as Huck was laid out, Jimmy and Harry stripped off his boots and pants and found he'd been shot in the left leg, upper thigh. There was no exit wound in the back of his leg, which meant the bullet was lodged inside.

They all turned when Tom screamed and saw that Maria was pouring whiskey into his wound. Tom, more concerned about Huck than himself, still hadn't lost his sense of humor, saying, "Maria, I don't even like to drink that stuff!"

In spite of everything, Maria smiled and poured a little more. She and Maddie then started with the bandages.

Sarah, distraught, turned to her father. "Is he going to be okay? Will he live?"

Without looking up, Jimmy answered, "He should be fine, but we've gotta get that bullet outta there before it becomes infected. Thing is, it's gonna hurt more coming out than it did going in."

Maddie, still working on Tom, asked, "Did he even feel it going in? He didn't say a word."

This time it was Harry who answered, "He knew he'd been shot. No man gets hit like that and doesn't know. But he also knew he had to finish those men out there and with Tom down, it was just the two of us, so he kept fighting. After that, he was more concerned about his friend than he was about himself. Jimmy, you probably already knew, but your Sarah got herself one hell of a man."

Jimmy looked at Sarah and then back down at Huck, as Harry continued.

"Seventeen? Most men I know twice his age couldn'ta done half a what he's done. Now, let's get this bullet out. I'm gonna need some hot, wet cloths, a knife—make sure it's cleaned with whiskey and fire—and then the bottle. Last thing. I'm gonna need a strong stick."

It didn't take long until Harry had everything he'd asked for. "We're gonna have to hold him down. This is gonna hurt like hell. Maddie, Maria, you hold his shoulders down. Jimmy, you're gonna have to hold both legs down. Not gonna be easy, but we don't have a choice. Sarah, you're gonna help me."

While everyone was focused on Tom and Huck, no one noticed that Cisco had worked his way out of the wagon and crawled over to where Huck was spread out on the ground. Maria started to say something but Cisco stopped her. "Been doing nothin' long enough. Jimmy, I can help you hold him down." He crawled the rest of the way and positioned himself so that he could hold down one leg.

Harry nodded at Cisco and lifted Huck's head. "Sarah, pour a little whiskey down his throat." She did. Huck drank some and spit some out. "Do it again."

Crying, Sarah did as she was told. Harry took the bottle from her and placed the stick in Huck's mouth. He then moved down to the leg.

He cleaned the wound with the hot cloth and then poured whiskey into the bullet hole. Huck would have screamed, but instead he bit down on the stick, exactly as Harry knew he would. He took the cleansed knife from Maria and started prodding the wound. Each twist of the knife was agony for Huck. Maria and Maddie had trouble holding him down, but they did. After what seemed like a very long time, Harry pulled out the knife, reached into the hole and pulled out the bullet.

Huck had passed out by now, so Harry kept working. He cleaned the wound again using the last of the whiskey as he did. Sarah gently removed the stick, which was just about bitten in half as Harry finished patching up the wound and Maddie and Maria turned their attention back to Tom.

Harry wrapped the leg and Jimmy helped him put Huck's pants back on. Then Harry and Jimmy helped Cisco, his face twisted in pain, back into the wagon. Tom propped himself up with his good arm and looked at his friend, asking Harry as he did, "Well?"

"He's gonna be fine, Tom. You both will." He looked over at Cisco. "I guess you all will."

Maddie asked, "What do we do now?"

Harry looked around at everyone, thankful that none of the women had been injured and realized that he was now the man in charge. Jimmy, sensing the change, looked at his friend and nodded and then Harry spoke.

"We've got a little more than a week before we roll into Bozeman. We'll stay here for a day, maybe two before we head out. It's not good, we're in the open on all sides, but we've got no choice. Can't risk Huck or Tom to start bleedin' again. Me and Jimmy'll split guard duties, and you," he said, looking at Sarah, Maddie and Maria, "will take care of the injured."

Maria was the first to answer. "No way the two of you can keep watch from here to Bozeman. You'll drop from lack a sleep." She looked at Sarah and Maddie and continued, "We'll pull our share. Before you say anything, you know I'm right."

Harry did start to speak, but Jimmy stopped him. "Harry, if you'd seen how fast these ladies grabbed rifles and started shooting, you'd know what she's saying is right. We can't stay awake for more than a week and we both know it."

Harry looked at each of the faces and could see the determination and the truth of what Maria and Harry had said. "I sheriffed for twenty years. Dealt with some of the meanest, orneriest cowboys, drunks and thieves you've ever seen, but I ain't never seen a group of people tougher than this one. I think we're all gonna be just fine."

# 31

## HAYES

IT WAS A LONG, restless, nervous night for everyone. Huck and Tom slept fitfully, but they did sleep. In the morning, everyone was pleasantly surprised that both men were awake and alert and that neither showed signs of infection or fever.

Perhaps the most pleasant surprise was Cisco, who was awake before anyone and was sitting up, on his own, looking around, rifle in hand. Maria looked concerned, but Cisco simply said, "It has been long enough and now with Tom and Huck..."

She understood and climbed down to start breakfast. Sarah and Jimmy rode in with the sun and while they both looked tired, they were happy to report that they had not seen or heard anything out of the ordinary. The early sun brought some welcome warmth and the day looked to be a pleasant one, at least as far as the weather was concerned.

Huck was the last to wake, but he had lost quite a bit more blood than Tom and the prodding to remove the bullet would take a bit to recover from. When breakfast was done, Tom surprised everyone. He used the wagon to pull himself upright and then stood without assistance.

"It won't do to sit around here. We were lucky yesterday that"—he looked at Huck and then at his own shoulder—"this was all that happened. We're just too exposed. Not enough grass for the horses and we'd be cuttin' our own food too close. Let's get Huck up in the wagon. I can ride. With Huck in the back, Sarah and Maria can take turns tendin' to 'em and sharing the reins with Maddie.

"Been thinking about it and I think all of us"—here he looked at Jimmy and Harry—"should stay close to the wagon all day. Worst thing is maybe me or Huck can't go all day, but no matter what, we'll be closer to Bozeman than we are now."

Huck joined in. "He's right. It'll be a couple a days before I can ride with this leg, but if we bandage it up tight, it won't bleed, same with Tom's shoulder. Cisco, you good to roll?"

Cisco smiled, something they hadn't seen in a while. "Yessir. Tom starts hurtin' too bad, feel like I could ride for a bit too." Maria's face made it clear that wasn't going to happen, but it was good to hear Cisco feeling better.

Harry and Maria worked on Tom's shoulder and Huck's leg while the others cleaned up and packed up. It took a bit to fit everything into the wagon with both Cisco and Huck needing to lie down, but they made it work. Sarah started off in the back, with Maddie and Maria sitting up front.

Sarah heard Maria say to Maddie, "About time I learned how to do this, so maybe you can teach me?"

Maddie handed her the reins and said, "Let's get started."

THE FIRST DAY they covered fewer than half the miles they normally would on flat ground, but that was because they stopped frequently to check on the three injured men and especially to see to the bandages. The day passed without incident and they stopped early for their final meal of the day.

They decided to all stay close to the wagon, so they took turns watching. Harry and Sarah took the first watch, Jimmy and Maddie the middle, and Cisco and Maria until dawn. It was the best Cisco had felt—and felt about himself—since the accident.

With each following day, they were able to put on more miles. On the fifth day, Huck rode for about an hour. Maria learned quickly and even enjoyed herself when she had the reins. On the same day that Huck rode for an hour, Cisco sat up front with Maria. Harry traded places with Sarah, who rode side by side with her father while Harry caught up on some much-needed sleep.

On the sixth day, as they were finishing up breakfast, they saw dust rolling toward them from the north. Fearing their good luck had run out, they prepared to defend themselves against whatever was coming their way. Jimmy, Harry and even Tom took to the horses. Huck, Cisco and the three women stayed with the wagon, all with rifles in hand.

The three men rode out to meet the newcomers and Jimmy wondered if they were ever going to get safely to their new home. They positioned themselves out in front of the wagon and waited.

It didn't take long before Tom said to the other two, "Looks like it's just a wagon. Don't see any other riders."

After a couple of minutes, he added, "Man and woman sittin' up front. Can't see anyone else." The men relaxed but didn't put their weapons away. The wagon eventually rolled to within a hundred yards of the three and the man pulled the wagon to a stop, stood up and yelled, "On our way to Casper. Not lookin' for any trouble."

The three men exchanged glances and Jimmy yelled back, "Not looking for any trouble ourselves. Headin' to Bozeman." The man in the wagon set down his rifle, climbed down from the wagon and started walking toward the three. Jimmy and Harry did the same. They met halfway between the horses and the wagon, where the man reached out his hand.

"Name's Hayes, Steve Hayes. That's my wife holding the reins. Her name's Connie. Children are tucked down in the wagon. Little Stevie and our baby girl, Molly."

Jimmy asked, "Where you headed, Mr. Hayes?"

"Currently? Casper. After that, back to Oklahoma Territory. Spent a winter up north and the wife hated it. Said she was going back to Oklahoma with the kids and I was welcome to join 'em. Didn't seem real open to talkin' about it, so here I am. We was just about to stop and eat. You folks care to join us?"

They did. They rolled the wagons up close. Little Stevie was seven, Enyeto's age, and Maria played with him for the entire two hours. Molly was only two and hung onto Sarah everywhere she went.

Huck marveled at how good she was with Molly and Tom whispered, "Looks like someone who's gonna be wantin' children soon." Huck would have hit him if he wasn't afraid of opening up his shoulder.

They stayed together for over two hours, long enough for Connie to delight Huck by baking some donuts. Steve told the men that there was nothing of note happening in Bozeman. They'd stayed for two nights and all was quiet. Harry and Jimmy pulled him aside and told him what had happened with the outlaws. Harry said the coyotes and buzzards should have taken care of the bodies by now, but he didn't want Steve to be surprised by what they would find.

Reluctantly, after everyone had eaten their fill and then some, both wagons packed up and headed in opposite directions.

Maria watched the Hayes' wagon and especially Little Stevie until she couldn't see them at all. She held Cisco's hand the entire time.

# 32

## BOZEMAN

Two days later, they rolled into Bozeman. Tom, Huck and Cisco were all feeling better, but everyone agreed staying a night or two was a good idea. Bozeman was the last stop and left them with a three-day trip to get home.

They rolled up in front of the Bozeman Café, which Huck and Tom remembered as having an excellent breakfast and a hotel attached. Huck, Tom and Cisco all managed, with a little help, to make their way up the boardwalk and take seats at a large round table in the restaurant.

Maddie and Sarah arranged for four rooms upstairs while Maria helped Harry and Jimmy unload what was needed from the wagon. Harry took the wagon and the horses to the livery, asking that the wagon be looked at one more time before the final push and the horses, who had worked hard for a long time, be given extra oats and a few healthy servings of corn.

He returned to the restaurant just as the food was being delivered. Huck had taken the liberty of ordering for the table, remembering how good the food had been last time. Harry took a seat as plates of fried eggs, ham steaks and pancakes were set down, quickly followed by biscuits and gravy, two loaves of bread with butter and honey, coffee, milk and orange juice.

The three injured men seemed to have found their appetites, which was a good sign. Even Maria was eating a full meal, something she hadn't done since the accident. Like a sailor who could smell the sea after an extended visit on dry land, all eight of them could sense how close they were to the end of this trip, this adventure, and the beginning of a new one.

Harry looked around the table and raised his glass of orange juice, offering a toast. "I know we have a few days left and I certainly don't take a safe trip for granted, but it most definitely feels as if we've left the worst of it behind. It has been hard." He stopped for a moment and looked at Cisco and Maria. "But we're here and all of us are starting new lives. It has been an honor to get to know each of you, and I look forward to building a new life—whatever that may be—with all of you."

Glasses and mugs clinked all around and when that was finished, Tom raised his coffee mug, standing as he did, and offered, "Here's to Enyeto. He will always be with those of us who knew him."

Tom sat down and Maria, who was sitting next to him, leaned over and gave him a kiss on the cheek. And then they all started eating. When the pangs of hunger were satisfied and the eating was for enjoyment, the conversation started back up again. Huck looked to Jimmy and Harry.

"There's a general store just a couple a doors from here. Man named Benjamin Thornberry runs it. Goes by Thorn. He knows me and knows the Circle CM. Maybe head down there and see if he has a wagon for sale. If he does, buy it and have him fill it. He knows what we're doing with the ranch and the new town, so just have him fill it with whatever he thinks we need. And make sure there's some things in there that'll make the women happy and some toys for the young ones. We've got credit there, so just be sure he knows it's for the CM."

Harry asked, "What kinds of things are you thinking about, Huck?"

"Building materials, any he's got. Cooking supplies. Beans. Sugar. Medicines. Maybe take Sarah and Maddie with you and they can pick out a few things for their new homes? Maria, is there anything you and Cisco need?"

Maria, feeling a little embarrassed, hesitated. Huck, sensing the problem, added, "Maria, you will always be family and even though you may be leaving in the spring, as long as you're here, you and Cisco are a part of the ranch, so whatever you need, you order it and don't worry about the money."

She reached across the table and without a word, took Huck's hand, tears in her eyes. With that, Harry, Jimmy and the three women stood up, excused themselves from the table and left to start their errands.

Tom looked at his two friends and smiled. "Well, we make one hell of a trio. Could barely make it from the wagon to the table and now that we're here, we're pretty useless."

Huck nodded and added, "We better heal up quickly. We all got plenty to do once we get to the ranch. Tom, you've got a woman to win over. Don't bother denying it—anyone who's seen you around her knows, and unless I miss my bet, she feels the same. A wildcat that one. She's gonna make you work for her hand, but I think she's worth it."

Tom mumbled his agreement.

Cisco looked at his two friends and said, "Don't know how I can earn my keep. Can't hardly walk and I've got no strength. Doesn't feel right."

Huck and Tom shared a look and then Huck spoke.

"Cisco, it wouldn't matter if you could never work again or if you never left the ranch. You long ago earned your keep with us. You and Maria have a place as long as you want one, be that forever or until next spring. Plenty a room and plenty a work for Cat and Clybs too, if they decide to come up—and something tells me they will. You're gonna get better and you're gonna have a kid. You worry about those two things and we'll take care of everything else. Spring'll come soon enough. No reason to be fretting about it now."

The conversation shifted to the new town and everything that needed to be done. The three of them enjoyed the conversation, the coffee and each other for over an hour until the others returned.

Huck watched as Maria, Sarah and Maddie laughed about something that had happened at the general store and Jimmy and Harry poured themselves a cup of coffee.

He wondered how he ever got so lucky.

# 33

## HOME

As anxious as everyone was to finish up the trip, they chose to spend three days in Bozeman. It was recuperative, physically and emotionally, for everyone. On the last night, the focus was on the future.

The eight settled down to have a nice meal and they were not disappointed. Roast pig, lamb chops, rabbit livers. Plenty of vegetables and bread and they even ordered two bottles of wine to celebrate. Jimmy was pouring but hesitated when it came to Sarah and her glass.

She looked at her father and laughed, saying, "Daddy, after all we've been through the last couple of months. With me getting married soon and all of us choosing to live in the middle of the wilderness, it's the wine you're worried about?"

As he slowly filled her glass, and after the laughter had

stopped, Jimmy spoke, quietly.

"I guess it was a little silly. But the thing is, you'll always be my little girl. Always. Even as I look at you now, I can see so much of your mother in you. Her beauty. Her spirit. Maybe you can forgive an old man for trying to hold back the changes he knows are coming.

"Ahh, hell, I know they're for the better. I love you and couldn'ta picked a better man than Huck. I'm excited about where we're going and what we're doing, but you're just gonna have to accept that in my eyes, you're still that same little girl that would run and jump in my arms and let me carry you around, pushing you on the old tree swing. So if you'll all raise your glasses, I'd like to say...

"Here's to the future. To Montana. To our new lives. To the joys and challenges that will be coming our way. And here's to my little girl. And to her mother, the woman who still brings me joy every day, even after all these years."

All the women started crying, while the men worked hard not to.

THE THREE DAYS since leaving Bozeman had been filled about talk of the future. Homes to be built, a ranch to run, a town to build. New families and old navigating their way through life. The three injured men continued to get stronger as if the very land itself was working as a cure.

Huck called for everyone to stop. They were at the bottom of a hill and Huck knew that from the top of it, they would look down into the valley, at the ranch house, the bunkhouse, the cattle and anything that had been built since he and Tom had left for Abilene.

Sarah had the reins of the wagon he and Cisco rode in and Maddie was handling the other wagon by herself. Tom insisted on riding horseback even though he was sore each night. Maria sat next to Cisco and Harry, and Jimmy rode in next to the wagons.

"We get to the top of this hill, you're going to be looking at your future. Wasn't so long ago, I stood there with my mother and father. I've never seen a place so beautiful and for those of you who haven't seen it yet, I hope you agree."

Huck then, slowly, worked his way from the back of the wagon to the seat up front. Sarah, smiling, offered him the reins, but he shook her off, saying, "You got us all the way here. You should be the one takes us to the top of the hill."

As they all started toward the top, Huck reached out and took Sarah's hand, the same way Brock did to Sophie the first time they rode up this hill. When they got to the top and looked down, Sarah gasped. She edged closer to Huck and tucked her head onto his shoulder.

Just like he did the first time he looked out from this hilltop, Huck knew he was home.

The End

# ALSO BY SCOTT HARRIS

**Brock Clemons Westerns**

Dry Springs Trilogy

*Coyote Courage*

*Coyote Creek*

*Coyote Canyon*

Grand Canyon Trilogy

*Mojave Massacre*

*Battle on the Plateau*

*Ambush at Red Rock Canyon*

Open Trails Trilogy

*Renegades*

*Return to Dry Springs*

*Deadly Trails*

Last in the Brock Clemons series

*Death in Abilene*

Companion Short Story Books

*Tales From Dry Springs*

*Tales From the Grand Canyon*


**Caz: Vigilante Hunter**

*Slaughter At Buzzards Gulch*

*Never Shoot A Woman*

*McKinley Massacre*

*Fire From Hell*

*Hell On Devil's Mountain*

*They Shouldn't A Killed Her*

**Stagecoach Willy**

*600 Bloody Miles*

*Wounded, Hunted & Alone*

*Death Across Texas*


**Six Clemons Modern-Day Western**

*Revenge on the Border*

*Juan Carlos Must Die*


**52 Weeks**

*52 Weeks * 52 Western Movies*

*52 Weeks * 52 Western Novels*

*52 Weeks \* 52 TV Westerns*

## 500 Word Micro Shorts

*The Shot Rang Out*

*A Dark & Stormy Night*

*Bourbon & A Good Cigar*

*Time To Myself*

## Western Adventures

*Grizzly Creek Runs Red*

*The Last Comanche*

*Coyote Junction*

## Plains: Short and Sweet

*Once Upon the Plains*

*Once More Upon the Plains*

*Back On the Plains*

## A Novel Journey – Writing Your First Western

## Six Gun Pardners – Collection of Father & Son short stories

## I Quit - First contemporary novel

Made in the USA
Columbia, SC
16 June 2023

18162225R00098